SET FREE

A Second Chance Small Town Novel

KELLY COLLINS

BOOK NOOK PRESS

Copyright © 2015 by Kelly Collins

No part of this publication may be reproduced, distributed, or transmitted in any form or by any means, including photocopying, recording, or other electronic or mechanical methods, without the prior written permission of the publisher, except as permitted by U.S. copyright law. For permission requests, contact kelly@authorkellycollins.com.

The story, all names, characters, and incidents portrayed in this production are fictitious. No identification with actual persons (living or deceased), places, buildings, and products is intended or should be inferred. All products or brand names are trademarks of their respective owners.

Dedication

To Jim, who roped my heart so many years ago.

Chapter 1

MICKEY

Today would be the last time I heard that lock engage. The last time I walked down the sterile corridor. And maybe the last time I'd see my friends.

Joy should pepper each step toward freedom, but sadness clouded my morning. Over my shoulder, the tear-stained faces of my closest friends stared. Survival had been a team sport. I blew a kiss to the remaining quartet and left Cell Block C behind.

The guard slapped a piece of paper on the cold metal counter and shoved a pen into my hand. "Ahem." He cleared the phlegm from his throat while he poked at the paper with his sausage-like finger.

Tucking the wild strands of hair behind my ears, I eyed it with suspicion.

"Sign here." His abrupt demeanor was expected. I was a number, another woman without value.

"What's this?" Squinting to read the fine print, it stated I was signing for my worldly goods. Goods that had not been returned to me. Without a signature, would they keep my stuff? If I refused, would they incarcerate me again?

Frustrated that I had so easily reverted to the scared girl, I shook my uncertainty off. What could they do to me that hadn't been done?

I had learned some valuable lessons in prison. Trust a few, fear the rest. Nope, there was no room in my life for the frightened, unsure Mickey of my past. I pushed the paper away in defiance. Firming my stance, I prepped for a confrontation.

"I'm not signing." I laced my fingers through my belt loop and with a tug, pulled up my pants and self-esteem. I pointed to a specific line on the paper. "It says right here that by signing this form, I acknowledge the return of my belongings, but you haven't given me my stuff back." My heart beat wildly in my chest. It was mere minutes until I was free to go home, where everything would return to normal.

Thick, pudgy fingers reached under the counter and pulled out a plastic bag. With a yank, the taped closure was ripped free. Recognizable items were dumped on the table.

He continued to stare blankly at the unsigned paper. The tapping of his fingers on the edge of the counter provided the tempo to which I worked. I took an inventory of my life.

Leather bag (black)
Wallet
Visa Credit Card
Visa Debit Card
Fifty-six dollars cash (2 twenties, 1 ten, 1 five, 1 one)
Twenty-two cents in coins (2 dimes, 2 pennies)
One set of keys (5)
Lip-gloss
iPhone

The inventoried items were placed into the expanding black bag. Getting cash back was a surprise. Didn't they write you a check?

"It's all here." To touch my belongings was liberating. With the pen firmly gripped, I signed my full name slowly and with a steady hand, which was in stark contrast to the tumultuous storm brewing inside me. What waited for me on the other side of the door? Would Morgan be there? I hadn't seen him since that night—the night that changed everything. I tamped down my fear and focused on my exit.

There were no words of encouragement. A button was pushed and the door behind me buzzed. "Don't let the door hit you on the way out," the guard said.

Stumbling backward, I grabbed the handle and catapulted myself outside. I didn't want to be trapped in this hellhole. I landed outdoors, and for the first time in a year, I was unsupervised.

I stood still on the top step, looking at the parking lot in front of me. Not used to living in autonomy, I waited for someone to tell me what to do.

Was there a proper way to exit prison and re-enter life? My subconscious eked out the words *one step at a time*. My heart boomed in my chest. I was frozen, paralyzed with fear. *You got this. This is easy.* How hard would it be to convince myself?

My shaky hand reached into my bag and pulled out the gloss to coat my rapidly drying lips. Pushing my unruly hair out of my eyes, I scanned the world around me.

The reinforced door blocked the portal to my past. I took the first tenuous steps in the only direction I could. Forward into my future.

Squinting into the brightness, I saw no one—nothing. Relief washed over me until I realized how alone I was. The emptiness around me seeped into my soul. What lay behind was not something I wanted to revisit, but venturing into the future was terrifying.

Inside the black bag, I searched for the phone. It didn't surprise me to find it completely dead. What surprised me was the system had dumped me on the sidewalk without so much as a phone call or a plan.

For me, it was irrelevant because there wasn't anyone to call, and I had no plan.

Out of order was written on a scrap of paper and taped over the coin slot of a nearby payphone. I hoped it wasn't a forewarning for the remainder of my life.

I resigned myself to hoofing it up the road. Step by step, I distanced myself from the prison. The farther I got, the better I felt.

My meager steps turned into long strides. My rounded shoulders straightened. With each step, the dirt I kicked up buried my past.

Twenty minutes later, the prison faded from view. The road ahead twisted and turned with nothing in sight. Leaving the confines of the Denver Women's Correctional Facility, I didn't expect my lack of resources to trap me in a new type of hell.

The sun sat high in the sky. I was well on my way to sunburnt limbs. Leaning against a signpost on the side of the road, I searched for cars leaving the prison. Maybe someone would be kind enough to give me a ride.

The hot breeze rattled the sign above my head. When I looked up, I laughed. It said *Correctional facility area. Do not pick up hitchhikers.* I continued on the dusty path, knowing that the universe had just flipped me off.

THE UNMISTAKABLE SOUND of tires on gravel filled my ears several steps later. A truck slowed down and pulled into the soft shoulder beside me. The dust billowed around my face, making me choke and cough in its wake.

The white Ford pickup idled quietly—waiting. Fear squeezed my throat like a noose tightening inch by inch. Could it be Morgan? I backed away while the window silently lowered.

"Do you need a ride?" the husky voice called from across the seat. It wasn't Morgan. So many emotions filled me.

Relief.

Fear.

Desire.

A sizzling energy threaded through every nerve in my body. It was a tingly zap of recognition. *Morse code for my libido? Electrocution by attraction?*

Looking into the clean truck and feeling the cool air seep out the window made it easy to take the risk. Without hesitation, I pulled on the door handle and hopped inside the truck.

Set Free

"Yes. Thanks. Being near the prison, I didn't think anyone would stop." I reached forward and turned the air vents to my face.

His inspection of me was short but thorough. The feel of his eyes sweeping across my body made the air around me crackle. It had been a long time since a man had seen me. Sure, the guards watched me daily, but they never actually saw me. I was a number, not a person.

The window rose, and the door lock engaged. The sound caused fleeting anxiety. Buckled into my safety belt, the truck propelled forward. I sat in the sexy stranger's car—captive.

"I wouldn't normally stop, but it's hell hot out there. I can't imagine walking anywhere in that heat. There aren't many who travel this direction, and I thought you might appreciate the lift."

The driver looked at me. I tensed. I was uncomfortable under his scrutiny without a stitch of makeup and my clothes falling off my too-thin body. Moving closer to the door, I whispered, "Thank you for stopping." I questioned if it was wise to climb in a truck with a stranger.

"Since you just got released from prison, it's unlikely you're armed and dangerous."

"How do you know I just got released?" Was it my look of desperation that clued him in? Did something happen to a person in prison that pegged them for life as the underbelly of society?

I tried desperately to get my hair under control, but there was only so much a girl could do when she hadn't had a cut or a good conditioning in over a year.

I pulled down the visor, hoping there wasn't a mystery tattoo across my forehead that said *ex-convict*. I was clean, my lips were shiny, and my skin was clear and smooth. All in all, what I saw in the tiny mirror wouldn't have sent anyone running in fear.

"I just finished interviewing an inmate when I saw you leave the building. The only people who leave that door are parolees or people who served their time. Which are you?" He glanced to his right, raised his brows and waited.

"I served my time. I'm free and clear." It felt good to have accomplished something, even if it was only a year in prison. Survival was always something to be excited about.

"You'll never be clear again, but you are currently free." He turned onto the main road, the roughened ride getting smoother with every mile we traveled. "Where do you need to go?"

"Anywhere there's a phone, so I can call a cab. They gave mine back, but it's dead."

"No need for a cab, I'll take you anywhere within a sixty-mile radius. I'd volunteer to go farther, but I have another interview later this afternoon."

"Interview?" The stiffness in my shoulders relaxed. The man appeared harmless. "Are you a reporter?" I peeled myself from the door and melted against the seat cushion.

"No, I work for Jefferson County. I'm Detective Kerrick McKinley. And who are you?"

A stifled groan slipped from my mouth before I could find restraint. I should have noticed the cocksure confidence that most cops have, but I was more interested in his air-conditioned truck than his occupation.

"I'm Michelle Mercer, but people call me Mickey. I live just outside of Lone Tree and would be grateful for the ride." I rotated my body so I could face him.

Now that I knew he was a cop, the spotless car didn't surprise me. After all, weren't cops known for being freaks of all types of cleanliness and control?

"I'm happy to drive you." His hands hung loosely around the steering wheel. "How long were you in prison?"

"I served a year." It was amazing how quickly a year could pass.

If my dad had been alive, I wouldn't be sitting comfortably on my behind. Even at my age, he would have taken his belt to my ass.

"What were you in for this time?" He turned onto Interstate 25 and drove south.

"This time?" My mouth fell slack at his audacity. "You make it sound like I'm some kind of habitual offender." *What the hell?* "This was my first and last brush with law enforcement."

There was an air of superiority that seemed to be bred into officers of the law. They must have some kind of arrogance training before they leave the academy. It seemed to be a required personality trait.

"I didn't mean to upset you, but most people have multiple offenses. So, as a liberated woman, what's the first thing you want to do?"

"I need to go to the grocery store to buy staples." I couldn't tell him I wanted to get laid, even though it was high on my priority list. Instead, I divulged my need for food. "There are so many things I'm craving right now." If I couldn't have a man buried deep inside me, then at least I could get a pint of ice cream.

After a cursory inventory, I decided he was an incredibly handsome man. Detectives must have a more lenient dress code than your average officer. His dark hair was nicely trimmed, but the scruff on his face was at least a week's worth of growth. Those bristly whiskers looked like they would leave a delicious burn between a girl's legs.

My friends who whispered all night about the things they missed about men created my obsessive sexual thoughts. Their scent. Their passion. Their...oh yes, their prowess.

Sex wasn't high on my priority list prior to incarceration, but I did miss men. Strange, but true. Now I found myself surprisingly aroused. So the itch needed scratching. Pronto. Naturally, seeing a hot man would bring those thoughts to the forefront of my mind.

The only thing non-appetizing about Detective McKinley was his career choice. Having spent a year in a cell, my opinion of public servants had changed. Not all officers of the law were looking to serve and protect.

His eyes were focused straight ahead, but I sensed his ears were completely tuned in to me. "So what's first on your list?"

"What?" My mind went straight to the gutter again. "You mean my list of cravings?"

"Yep, what are you craving?" Being a detective, he had to have noticed the waver in my voice.

"Ice cream is a must, followed by summer fruits like fresh

peaches, pears, and plums." Excess saliva filled my mouth at the mention of my favorite foods.

"Don't they serve fruit in prison?"

My nose wrinkled at the thought of prison fruit. "Yes. Canned. If we got fresh fruit, it was bananas or apples." I mentally promised myself to never eat fruit cocktail again.

"It's amazing what we take for granted. Listen, I can take you to the grocery store in Lone Tree. You can tell me how to get to your house when we're finished shopping."

"You don't have to do that. I have a truck at home." I stared out the window and hoped someone at the ranch had had the forethought to drive it during the year. "It should be fine provided someone's been using it. Worst-case scenario, the battery is dead." Thinking about the ranch, I wondered what Michael and Andrew would think when I pulled up. They had to know I was coming home today. Why didn't they come and get me?

"It's not a big deal, I have to pick up a few items myself." He ran his hand over his prickly face. "I need razor blades." His fingers crossed over his rugged jaw. Strong desire spread through me and settled between my thighs. I didn't know this man, and yet I was fantasizing about rubbing his face all over my body.

"Don't shave. I like that look on you. It's masculine and sexy." *Shit, I just told him he was sexy. What the hell was I thinking?* I had to work on my game.

My gaze shifted from his facial hair down his muscled arms. The white polo shirt strained against his golden brown, bulging biceps. I was a hummingbird thirsty for his nectar.

One thing was certain, sex couldn't be put off for long. I'd had a year of celibacy before my incarceration, so it had been a *long* time.

As the truck came to a halt in front of the store, I threw the door open with abandon. My boots hit the pavement with a thud. The simple act of exiting a vehicle was freeing. With a swift push, I shut the door and took a step toward feeling normal.

Kerrick followed closely behind me. The automatic doors opened to a playground of opportunity and choices. Every color of the rainbow was present in the massive produce displays. Oranges and red apples, sun yellow bananas, and purple grapes were overflowing the bins. Pushing the shopping cart in front of me, I entered a wonderland.

"The food must have been awful where you were staying. I've never seen anyone light up over produce."

Only the burgundy and grey of my prison uniform had filled my sights for the past year. But here the full-color palette spread before me was extraordinary.

"It was beyond bad." I went straight for the peaches. The flesh gave slightly under my fingers, the scent of summer filled me. Perfection.

"How do you know if it's ripe?" He sidled up next to me while I placed my selected fruit into the cart.

His whiskey-brown eyes focused on me while I told him my secret. "I like to squeeze them a little. If the flesh gives in, then I know it's ripe. The other test is to smell it. If it smells like you would want it to taste, then I buy it."

His eyes sparkled with mischief while a lustful smile took up residence on his face. "There are a lot of things I smell, and in turn want to taste, but I might get arrested if I licked every sweet-smelling girl I came in contact with." He turned and disappeared down a nearby aisle, returning moments later with a package of razor blades and a six-pack of soda.

Lost in the thought of him licking me, I stood still in the aisle wondering why I was thinking such dirty thoughts? A vision of his tongue on my bare breasts sent a hot sensation across my skin.

"Can I help you locate anything that won't give you pleasure to pick out?" His words spoken softly and way too close to my ear broke me out of my daydream. "I'm sure there are items like laundry detergent and cleaning supplies that aren't exciting to choose."

The talk of laundry and cleaning supplies wiped away the thoughts of his tongue. *Almost.*

"Honestly, it all sounds rather exciting." I wanted to sniff the cleaners and squeeze the toilet paper. "Do you have any idea how rough prison toilet paper can be?" Rolling my eyes, I pushed forward. "No, of course, you don't."

We breezed through the produce section and headed to the butcher. Two chunky pieces of salmon were placed in my cart. I was excited to have fish not shaped like a domino. We weren't all Catholics, but fish was served every Friday like it was lent.

Next was cleaning supplies. The smell of Pine Sol floated through the air. I closed my eyes and inhaled. Lemon-scented cleaners triggered memories of my mother. Blair used to sprinkle Pine Sol around the house when she didn't have time to clean. She said it made the house seem cleaner, if only in her mind.

On to feminine hygiene. I tried to inconspicuously lift the jumbo box of tampons from the shelf. It was embarrassing to show a man you didn't know your brand, but if he wanted to follow closely, he'd get treated to the full experience.

Making my way down the aisle, I reached for a bag of disposable razors. I weighed my options and chose the cheaper brand.

"Put those back." His tone could make a small girl shake in her boots. "They'll tear up your legs. Go for the better brand. You won't regret it."

Startled, I distanced myself by moving across the aisle. "The better brand costs more than my salmon." Although I argued my point, I shoved the bargain brand back into the slot and went for the expensive pink blades. "Besides, who says I'm shaving my legs?" The look on Kerrick's face was priceless. "Get your mind out of the gutter. I'm shaving my armpits. However, I may just have to shave the other. I hear men love that." I propelled the cart forward with a gentle push, leaving him behind.

He was a lot of fun to tease, but his rough demeanor needed an overhaul. I slowed down so he could catch up. He walked to my side, leaned over and whispered in my ear.

"I've never been a fan of a shaved pussy, but I can see the advantages." He pulled the razors from the cart and inspected them. "I don't mind a good flossing when I go down on a woman, but I don't want to be face deep in Sasquatch either." He tossed the package back. "There's nothing wrong with a good trim."

Surprised by his boldness, I came to a stop and turned toward him. His eyes narrowed in my direction. His bottom lip was pulled seductively between his teeth. I stared at his lip while he chewed it gently.

My mouth became as dry as day-old toast, and I couldn't take my eyes off his lips. Oh, to have his lips on me, the possibilities were endless. To nibble on or nibble with...

After a sly wink, I asked, "Are you playing with me, Officer McKinley?" I walked forward, listening for his answer.

"It's Detective McKinley." His stern voice demanded attention. "I won't have you demote me before you get to know me."

"Am I going to get to know you, Detective?" Something about him was captivating. It could simply be that he'd been nice to me. Nice felt sexy.

"Without question." His answer held a promise of something to come. He pulled the cart from my hand and pushed forward at a brisker pace. "What else do you need? I still have to get to my interview."

He cruised through the aisles of the supermarket, tossing items into my cart. Pinto beans and canned spinach. Corned beef hash and Spam. He pitched items in the cart like he was on a game show and his time was running short.

"Hey, what are you doing?" I removed the box of chocolate cupcakes, but he covered my hand with his. "Some of the things you're putting into my cart have no nutritional value. Empty calories." His large palm dwarfed mine completely.

"Did those pants fit you when you went away?" My jeans seemed to wilt under his gaze.

I yanked on the belt loop. "Yes, but the food in prison turned my stomach, so I didn't eat much." I didn't eat, I didn't sleep, I didn't dream. There were no thoughts of cupcakes, candy bars, or sexy men.

"You need those empty calories. Women are so much more fun to play with when they have a little meat on their bones."

I let the cupcakes drop back into the cart. "I didn't think you played." After living with one hundred forty female inmates for the past twelve months, it felt good to have a male around. His masculinity was making me crazy.

"Oh, don't be mistaken. I play, in fact, I play long and hard, but I don't play *around*. No games for me. Expectations are always clear." He tossed a few more boxes of junk food into the cart and guided it through the frozen food section.

Two rows later, I whooped with joy. I'd arrived at heaven on earth. There was an entire row dedicated to ice cream. If he wanted me to devour countless empty calories, I'd prefer to have them by the quart. Armed with a week's worth of ice cream, I rolled my nearly full cart to the register.

Recognition fluttered across the face of the cashier. She seemed familiar, but I couldn't be certain why. The bleached blonde stared at me while she scanned the groceries.

Kerrick stood to the right with his hand basket of soda and razors. I pulled his items out and placed them next to mine. It was a small payment for the ride.

He reached for them, but I placed my hand on top of his and shook my head.

Blondie interrupted the moment. "I thought it was you." She leaned in to get a better look. "I thought you were—"

"I was, but I'm finished now." A rosy blush of embarrassment bled across my face. For whatever reason, I'd not taken my hand from his.

He eyed the woman and then turned his hand to hold mine. Out of my element, I took the comfort he offered. I needed his strength. Even if it were only a finger hold, I'd hang by my nails if I had to.

"Your total is $168.13," the cashier said, her eyes traveling from Kerrick's hand to my face. "How do you always get the sexiest men?"

Her question perplexed me. How would this woman know who I'd dated?

"It's a curse," I said with no humor in my voice. I reluctantly pulled my hand away and reached into my wallet to get my debit card. Although I was fresh out of prison, I knew everything would be okay. It was reassuring to know I had a home, business, and money. I pulled the card through the reader, the friction creating a squeak.

"Run it again. It came back denied," the cashier blurted. "That happens sometimes, especially with cards that haven't been used in a while." She was talking to me, but her gaze was glued to Kerrick.

After running it again, the machine shouted its denial with quick successive beeps and a flashing banner.

With limited options, I pulled out my credit card and slid it through the machine. *Denied* flashed across the screen. It was bad enough to not be able to pay for the groceries I'd lovingly picked out, but to appear broke and destitute in front of Kerrick was intolerable. Even though I'd just met the man, I liked him, and his opinion of me mattered.

My heart sank into the pit where my self-respect resided. I reached for the cash I had on hand, but it wouldn't cover the bill. I pulled some of the groceries from the bag.

"Honey, I'm sorry. I forgot to give you your new cards." Had he lost his ever-lovin' mind? He called me honey, and then he handed the cashier his credit card. He pressed a kiss to my forehead before loading the bags into the cart. He glowered at the cashier before he turned to walk away. My legs had to do double time to keep up. He tossed the bags into the bed of the truck before he opened the door for me.

When he entered the driver's side, I spewed my apologies. "I'm sorry. I don't know what happened. When I went to prison, I had a lot of money in my account. The ranch makes money. I accounted for the monthly bills. Even if the ranch was dead broke, I had enough money to pay for everything and still have several thousand dollars left when I returned. You have to believe me." I pulled the $56.00 from my purse and laid it on the seat beside him. "I'll pay you back, Kerrick. I promise."

"I know you will. I'm not worried about it. Hell, I put half the stuff in your cart." The money sat untouched between us. "Mickey, your accounts are probably inactive. It will take a visit to the bank to straighten things out, but I'm sure it'll be fine." He reached over and grabbed my hand. I had only just met this man, yet he'd given me a ride, bought me groceries, and now he was holding my hand. *Was he for real?*

"You seem angry at me." My voice turned to a whisper, and I shrank in my seat.

"I'm not mad at you. I'm mad at the cashier. She treated you like you had no value. That irritates me." He punched the power button on the radio, blanketing us in silence.

"I've had lots of people discount my value lately." Unsure of what else to say, I filled the uncomfortable silence with reassurance. "I have money at the ranch. I left it in the safe. My dad always told me to have cash on hand for emergencies. This counts."

After an awkward pause, he responded, "Your dad is a smart man." He patted my hand reassuringly before he put his hand back on the steering wheel.

"Yes, he was. He's been gone two years." I stared at the dashboard in front of me. My focus was far away. *Had it really been that long since he died?*

"It sounds like it's been a tough couple of years for you. I'm sorry for your loss. I know what it feels like to lose someone you love."

I mumbled my response. "He didn't come home from a fence check. I rode out in search of him and found him on the lower third of our property. He was already gone."

"I'm sorry, Mickey. That must have been awful for you. You said the ranch. Is that where we're going?"

I nodded my head. Picking at a frayed hole on the knee of my jeans, I struggled to understand why things had to be so tough and painful.

"Take Country Road D to Longview, and then take a left into M and M Ranch. That's where I live." A lone tear snuck down my cheek and plopped onto the back of my hand.

"I know the ranch. You own that land?" He put the truck in reverse, and our journey continued.

"I own most of it. Eighty percent is mine, the other twenty

percent belongs to the foreman. My dad thought he was a good guy."

"Was he?" He cocked his head in question, before turning his attention to the road. We were minutes from my home.

"No." There was nothing to say on the matter.

He took the turn onto Longview and drove under the wooden pillars that held the massive M and M Ranch sign. The yucca-dotted land had been in my family for over a century.

In the distance, the buildings came into view: my house, stables, barn, and cabins were all there.

Would Morgan be there? Apprehension ripped through me as we approached the main house. The grass in front was knee high. The paint was beginning to peel. It was a complete mess, but what could I expect?

My truck sat in the driveway in one piece. No slashed tires. No broken windows. *Whew.* I walked slowly to the front door. What greeted me was the emotional equivalent of a brutal punch to the gut. *Could my day get any worse?*

Chapter 2

MICKEY

I entered the house with trepidation. *What the hell happened?* I'd expected to walk into a place that felt familiar, warm, welcoming. Instead, I faced the remnants of what used to be my home. A mountain of furniture in the center of the room. Shards of glass strewn across the floor. My throat tightened. My eyes stung with unshed tears. My heart pounded in my chest. Spray-painted on the far wall in big block letters was FUCKING BITCH!

Morgan was always short on words and big on drama.

Kerrick whistled. "It's a bit on the edgy side, but I love how you've decorated the place."

His attempt at humor worked. I shook my head and laughed. If this was the worst Morgan had done, then I felt lucky.

Deep inside, I had a horrible feeling this was just the beginning.

We walked through the house cautiously, tiptoeing over the broken glass on our way to the kitchen. Kerrick had several bags of groceries in his hands he placed on the counter. Thankfully, the kitchen was virtually untouched. The only sign of anyone having been there was a dirty glass and an empty bottle of Jack Daniels.

"Do you have any idea who would do this to your house?" He

glanced around the place once more. "Call the police. I'll stay until they get here."

"I don't need to call the police. I know exactly who did this." I unpacked the bags that contained refrigerated goods. "He's holding a grudge, and I'm paying the price for a minute of poor judgment."

"This seems like a large debt to pay for a moment of stupidity." His eyes lingered just a bit too long on the bold words scrawled across the wall. The intensity of his expression left me feeling edgy —unsettled.

"I didn't say I was stupid, I said I made a poor choice." I tossed the canned goods in the cabinet. "I'm a bit impulsive, and in this case, it came back to bite me in the ass."

"Do you want to look around the outside?" His eyes burned with questions. "I can go with you to the stables to check on the horses and stuff."

"No, it's okay, I'm afraid to look. Things are not what I'd hoped they'd be. I think it's best if I feed myself disappointment in small doses."

"All right, then. I have to go to my interview." He walked slowly around the pyramid in the center of the room. "But I'll come back later and help you clean up." His detective's eyes scanned for clues.

Shoring up my courage, I walked confidently into the living room. Spreading my hands out wide, I said, "This is something I can handle. It's just a bit of cleanup. Once I finish with this, my next priority is to get good and drunk. Where would you suggest I do that?" I tried to remain calm in spite of the knot that twisted inside my stomach. This was not the homecoming I'd envisioned.

The tightness of Kerrick's jaw was evidence of his displeasure.

"Do you think going out and getting drunk is the answer?" He gave me a look that shouted, *Not gonna happen.* "You just got out of prison, and I'd bet getting drunk isn't the way to go."

"I haven't had a drink or a dance in over a year." I shimmied to imaginary music. "The last time I had physical contact with the opposite sex was when I slashed my ex's tires and beat him with a tire iron. That action didn't elicit a romantic response. Besides, I promised Holly, Megan, Natalie, and Robyn I'd toss back a shot of tequila for each of them." I teared at the thought of my friends still locked in Cell Block C. "They're counting on me."

"Do you think they'd want you to end up back in jail because you acted irresponsibly? I'm assuming these girls are from the prison?" His lips stretched into a thin line that resembled unhappiness. "How do you plan to get to this bar and toss back at least four drinks, then get home? I can't let you drive drunk."

"Why do you care?" *What was with this guy?* "What I do is up to me, but I'll take a cab if it makes you feel better." *The man was hot, but he wasn't my parole officer.*

"I'll pick you up and take you to Tommy's. You can get rip-roaring wasted if that's what you want, because I'll make sure you get home safely."

"Why?" I didn't understand his need to take care of me.

"I don't know why. This isn't standard behavior for me. I've never picked up a hitchhiker or helped a felon. I'm typically on the other side of the law—you know, the right side." His chest stretched the tight confines of his shirt. Each breath seemed to feed his imposing stature.

If he weren't so cute, I might have beaten him over the head. I had wickedly good aim when it came to a metal bar to the side of the head.

"Hey, it was a class-one misdemeanor with a side of justified assault, and I wasn't hitchhiking. You pulled over and offered me a ride." He had a way of making me feel fabulous and filthy in the same sentence. In the right circumstances, that could have been intriguing.

"I've been corrected on both counts. Be ready at seven," he said sternly. He gave my house another glance before he walked out the door, removing any opportunity for argument.

His white truck quickly disappeared, leaving a dust cloud behind. Back in the house, I surveyed the damage. It looked worse than it was. This was fixable, my finances were questionable.

Whatever happened to my bank account was not an accident. How Morgan managed to pilfer every dime I had was beyond my

Set Free

imagination. I couldn't stop the sinking feeling that every bad thing that had happened would point straight to him. Bad happened the day he showed up.

Thankfully, I'd never revealed the safe in my room. It was the one thing that belonged to me.

Fighting the need to check my bed for snakes and spiders, I walked timidly across the bedroom and crept toward the bed. Morgan would have been the only snake to sleep there, and I wouldn't put it past him to try and kill me off with a poisonous, slithering creature.

I stood to the side and yanked down the bedding and screeched. Thankfully, there was nothing but dust and the stale smell of old sheets. I quickly ripped them off and remade the bed. Even doing that felt cathartic, redeeming somehow.

I tossed the old sheets in the hamper and walked to the closet. The shoe rack scraped noisily across the wooden floor as I tugged it. The lock clicked open when I entered the final number to the combination. Relief washed over me as the door sprung free and revealed the large stack of cash.

Heavy in my hand, I counted out the hundred dollar bills one at a time. One hundred, two hundred…five hundred…four thousand…eight thousand, until the last bill had been counted. Comforted with the knowledge I wasn't completely destitute, I slid three hundred dollar bills into my pocket and locked down my life savings.

Broken glass and overturned furniture was next on the to-do list. Glass shards fell from the photos I picked up from the floor. The saddest thing about the vandalism was the damage to the only pictures I had of my mother and father. Scratches marred their faces, but their smiles were still visible. A whoosh of air blown from my mouth scattered the remaining specks of glass before I gently placed the photos on the table.

With the furniture in its upright position, I muscled it into place and collapsed on the soft sofa. Dust bunnies floated in the light that peeked through the window. I closed my eyes and envisioned better times.

The crew used to hang out in this living room after a long day. The door was always open, and the beer was always cold. We were all family in the business of raising cattle. Every face flashed through my memory as I turned the pages of the mental scrapbook of my life. Where were they now?

It took the better part of the morning to organize the house. The smell of pine and lemon filled the air. With the exception of the painting on the wall, it almost felt like home. The only thing missing was people.

Next on the list was ice cream. Two scoops of pralines and cream filled the bowl in my hands. I strolled into my office and turned on the computer. While it powered up, I called the bank.

"Good afternoon, this is Michelle Mercer. There seems to be a problem with my account." I prayed no one would put me on hold. My life had been on hold for the last year. "Is there someone who can help me?"

"Certainly, Ms. Mercer. My name is April Donovan. Do you have your account number?" She sounded pleasant enough, and I was thrilled to be talking to a real person.

"Yes, it's 71873014." It was funny how a person remembered certain things. Addresses, phone numbers, and prisoner IDs would always come easy.

"I'll need you to verify your birth date and address, please." Feeling grateful I wasn't set aside, I happily rattled off the data Ms. Donovan requested.

The information rolled off my tongue with ease. It felt good to not say Denver Women's Correctional Facility as my place of residence.

"Your account went delinquent over a month ago. There is an overdraft of $1000 due."

"I don't see how that's possible." My pitch rose with each word. "I had left over $40,000 in the account before I went away for the year, and all my bills were on auto pay. How can I be overdrawn by $1000?" With my heart in my stomach, I tried to process this new setback.

"I can't give you detailed information over the phone, but if you want to come in tomorrow and settle your account, I can have the transactions for the last year printed for you." It was clear no information would be given until I paid the overdraft.

"You can ask for my account number, but you can't divulge account information over the phone. That's insane." I scooped a large spoonful of ice cream into my mouth.

"I'm sorry, Ms. Mercer, there's too much information to give over the phone. I can't break the rules. When can you come in?"

I understood the concept of rules. I'd been living by an interesting set of them for the past year. I couldn't fault the woman for wanting to keep her job.

"I can be there around one o'clock." I listened to the noise created by fingers tapping against a keyboard. "Do I ask for you when I arrive?"

"Yes, I put you on my calendar. Would you like me to send you an e-mail reminder?" She waited patiently for me to respond. It was a nice gesture, but it wouldn't do any good. If there hadn't been any money in the account for over a month, then all services like the Internet and cable were long gone.

"No, thanks. I'll see you tomorrow."

Cold ice cream soothed my hot temper. I scraped the bowl of the remaining candied nuts and ground them into a fine powder between my clenched teeth. The spreadsheet in front of me confirmed what I already knew to be true. There had been plenty of money in the account to cover any expenses that came up. The only variable was an open account at the local farming supply store. Either an expensive piece of equipment needed to be replaced or someone was having a good time at my expense. My gut told me it was the latter, but I was hoping I was wrong. I wanted to believe everything was going to be okay. *But would it?*

I had an obligation to visit the ranch houses and let everyone know I was home, but I decided to hole up for another day. I needed time to adjust to my freedom. Tonight I'd blow off steam, tomorrow I'd dive back into business.

The crew had to know I was scheduled to return. Morgan was notified of my impending release at least a week ago as part of his victim's rights. It was probably why he was nowhere in sight. Instead, he left me a spray-painted welcome home note. That was more than I wanted from him.

Laughter erupted as I thought about being the aggressor. At five-foot-six and one hundred thirty-five pounds soaking wet, I was strong for a gangly girl, but no match for Morgan's two hundred thirty pounds of beef-fed brawn.

The night I was arrested, I had a bloody nose and a broken rib, but between the evidence and the witness statements, it was a cut and dried case. It didn't help that Morgan's second cousin oversaw the sentencing. I blew through the system like a leaf in a windstorm. I went from arrest to the Denver Women's Correctional Facility in record time.

Thinking about Morgan gave me a slimy, dirty feel, so I headed to the bathroom to enjoy a long, hot shower with skin-softening soap and shampoo that smelled like mango and coconut. The feel of my bare feet against the slick bathtub was wonderful. Turning in my shower shoes had been one of the high points of my day.

The razors Kerrick had suggested were amazing. They glided over my calves, leaving my skin smooth and supple. Thinking about his comment on shaven pussies gave me a giggle. I had done that once for Morgan and spent the next week scratching myself raw as the hair grew back. I'd never again give in to the silly sexual whims of a man. I exited the steamy bathroom in search of clothes.

Looking through my options, I realized looking sexy would be limited by the weight I had lost. Dropping down to one hundred twenty pounds left almost nothing in my closet that fit. Even my shoes were loose. How was I supposed to succeed at priority number one if I dressed like a fashion reject? Somehow, I managed to pull something together before the bell rang.

He arrived precisely at seven o'clock. I swung the door open wide and nearly lost my balance when I saw the man in front of me. In black jeans and a snug-fitting gray shirt, he was dressed to dazzle women and intimidate men.

I reached up to brush my fingers against his jaw. "You didn't shave." The hair was softer than I expected. Letting my fingers linger against his chin, his eyes flashed with mirth.

He pulled my palm down his rugged jaw and placed my fingertips to his mouth. His full lips puckered against my knuckles. My runaway heart beat a path south to my neatly trimmed center.

"You have my razors and my soda." He scanned me from top to bottom. "Are you ready?" he asked. "I figured I'd take you to Tommy's first, but if you don't like it there, we can shift to Rick's Roost." He held my elbow and pulled me out the door.

"Yes, I'm ready, but I need you to come in for one second. I have your money." I turned around and led him into the house. He inhaled sharply as I walked away. Self-conscious, I pulled at my short dress, hoping it hadn't ridden up too far. Maybe belting it at the waist wasn't such a good idea. Without the belt, the dress had the hallmarks of a potato sack. No shape or definition. With the belt, it became something slightly longer than a mini. "Do you think my dress is too short?"

"Yes, it's definitely too short for my comfort zone, but you look sexy." His eyes took me in once more. "Maybe I should go home and pick up my weapon. I'm not packing tonight, but maybe I should be." There was something in the depth of his gaze. Did I see appreciation? "It looks like I might be pulling men off you all night." That was a dizzying thought.

"Maybe I don't want you to pull the men off me. Do you have any idea how long it's been since I've had a man *on* me?" *Did I say that out loud? Hell.* Blushing at my lack of verbal restraint, I picked up my purse and pulled out two one hundred dollar bills. When I turned around, I saw his jaw tense and his shoulders tighten.

"I don't want to know." His voice was gruff and unyielding. "I just want to make sure you don't end up back in prison by tomorrow. Let's go." He turned on his heel and walked to the front door.

With one backward glance, I walked out the door wondering what in the hell I'd said to make him so angry. I tucked the bills into his front jeans pocket as I passed and walked straight to his truck.

"Aren't you going to lock the door?" He stood next to my front door and stared at me. "You have keys, right?" he asked before he twisted the lock.

"Yes, I have keys, but I've never locked the door. I've never had to." He locked the house and walked toward the truck. "My dad always had an open-door policy, and I've maintained that." He opened my door and helped me inside before he ran around the truck and entered.

"New rules. You lock the door. Even if you're home and feeling safe, you need to lock the door at all times. Someone doesn't write *fucking bitch* on the wall when they're feeling warm and fuzzy about you. Whoever did that is not feeling particularly fond of you."

"When did you become my big brother? I can take care of myself." I twirled a strand of brown hair around my finger.

"Oh, yes, that's quite evident by the fact you just got out of prison. You're obviously a model citizen, a perfect example of good judgment." He tapped his thumb against the steering wheel and fidgeted with the radio. We drove off the property with the song "Brand New Day" by Sting playing in the background. *How apropos.*

Apart from not having to walk the many miles home, I'd had a shitty day. *How dare he judge me?* "You're an ass." My anger and voice rose quickly. "I didn't ask for your help, but I'm grateful you offered. However, if you're going to sit here and judge me, especially when you don't know me, then I'd rather take a cab and go by myself." My hands slipped protectively across my ribcage as I curled into the seat.

"You're right, I don't know you, but here's what I do know. I know you got out of prison and plan to tie one on tonight. I know I'm not letting you go back to jail. I know someone is pissed at you. You have a big issue with your bank account. Your house was trashed. You're too skinny. Your ranch is in trouble, and you need a friend. What else do you want me to know?"

I sat in silence, looking out of the window. He knew a lot more than I would have liked, but he didn't have a clue as to *who* I really was. "I'm not who you think I am. I'm a good person who got caught in a bad situation. I made a bad decision, and I paid for it. In fact, I'm still paying for it. Can't I pretend everything is perfect tonight? I want to be a normal person with normal problems, enjoying a normal night out. Tomorrow is a different story. Can we do that?"

There was a pregnant pause before he answered. "I can live with that, but tomorrow you need to begin to straighten your life out. Did you call the bank?"

I couldn't understand why he was so concerned with my well-being. He was a virtual stranger, and yet he acted like he had a vested interest in my future.

"Why. Do. You. Care?" I turned in my seat to face him. His jaw was set, the tension visible in the sharp muscles that jutted below his cheekbones.

"I don't care, but it has to be done. Did you call them?" His tone was unrelenting.

Resigned to answer his question, my head fell forward and I said, "Yes. Apparently, while I was on my year-long sabbatical, my account had been sucked dry. I have an appointment tomorrow. The bank is printing all the statements so I can look them over. I would have done that today, but I no longer have cable or Internet."

"Who did this to you?" His voice softened as he spoke. "I've been trying hard not to press where I'm not invited, but I can't pretend I didn't see your house in complete disarray." We drove toward the orange glow of the setting sun.

"My best guess would be Morgan Canter, the foreman on the ranch and my ex-boyfriend." I let out a frustrated sigh. "I really don't want to talk about him right now. Can't we have a pleasant evening?" I stared out the window as we drove along.

"Let's have a good time, then. You'll eat first, and then you can drink. You won't get a drop of alcohol until you put something in your stomach. By the way, what did you eat today? And don't tell me ice cream."

Staying silent was all I could do. If he didn't want to hear ice cream, then I couldn't say a word.

"Mickey, you have to eat," he grumbled.

"I was busy. It's not like I'm intentionally starving myself. I was intent on getting my house back in order so I could live there. I wasn't thinking about my stomach. I was more concerned about finding out if the bastard robbed my safe and drained my account." I reached up to scratch the tingle spreading across my scalp.

"I thought we weren't going to talk about him," he reminded me.

I threw my hands in the air and shook my head. My hair fell around my shoulders and settled on top of my breasts.

Riding in silence, his eyes kept sliding to the one curl that rested on the curve of my breast.

Tommy's parking lot was packed, but he found a space close to the door. Kerrick ran around the truck and helped me exit. Tucking my arm in his, he walked me into the busy bar. Music played loudly from the jukebox. It wasn't a song I recognized, but it had a nice beat. I had an entire year's worth of music to investigate.

Breaking free from Kerrick's grip, I headed straight for the bar and slapped a one-hundred dollar bill on the counter. I asked the bartender for five shots of top-shelf tequila. I felt a tug at my elbow and swung around to see the dark intensity of Kerrick's eyes.

"Eat first, drink second." He pulled me toward a vacant table and helped me into a seat. "What the hell do you not understand about putting something in your stomach before you pickle your liver?" Irritation seeped out of him like a slow, controlled leak. His temper was in check, but I studied him with caution.

The last thing I needed was another explosive male on my hands. Morgan was a powder keg, and it didn't take much to ignite his temper.

I glanced around to find all available exits. I'd learned early on to have an escape plan in case things went south. The bar was full, the dance floor loaded. Neon signs advertised everything from beer to wine to the exit.

I felt safer with Kerrick than I had with Morgan, but a temper was a temper. I wanted to tell him to fuck off and leave me alone, but I wasn't that brave. I had no idea how he would react. With a growl, I pulled a menu from the end of the table. "I understand you fine. I'll eat, but I want my shots."

"Do you like burgers?"

I pulled my lips until they stretched thin.

"Answer me, Mickey, or you're getting whatever I decide you need to eat. It may be something you don't like." He scanned the menu, and I feared he was searching for the most repulsive thing he could find.

"Yes. I like cheeseburgers, hamburgers, French fries, and onion rings," I snapped. Picking up the napkin from the table, I proceeded to shred it into tiny pieces. Kerrick walked to the bartender and placed our order. He returned with a small tray containing five shots of tequila and what appeared to be a soda. He placed the tray just out of reach and lined up the shots in front of him.

"Tell me about the women these drinks represent." He tapped the five glasses one by one.

With my eyes focused on the first drink, I sat for a moment in quiet contemplation. What was I supposed to tell a detective about women who were still sitting in prison? It wasn't like he was going to see the value of their friendships or understand how many women were victims of their circumstances.

Half of the women I met while in prison would honestly say they were guilty of their crimes, but it was the circumstances surrounding those crimes that needed to be explained and taken into consideration before sentencing.

"For example, whose drink is this?" He lifted the shot on the far right.

"That drink is for Holly. She's twenty-seven and serving a two-year sentence for possession of marijuana with intent to sell. She wouldn't have to serve a day if she were pulled over now. The legalization of pot changed everything. She's not innocent, she had the drugs, and although she didn't intend to sell them, she did get them for her mother, who was dying of cancer. Sadly, her mom passed while she was in prison. She has a few more months until her sentence is finished. She'll be reuniting with her fiancé. They were supposed to get married in June."

He sat for a moment in silence. "Has she had much contact with her fiancé?"

"Not as much as she would like. Do you think things will have changed too much for them?" With my elbows on the table, I cradled my head and stared at the drinks like a hungry dog staring at a bone.

"I have no idea. A lot can happen in two years." His expression lacked the confidence he'd displayed all day. "I hope it works out for her." I did, too, but in what world would a man wait two years for a woman?

"Me, too. I'm hoping she'll come stay on the ranch for a while. It's a good place to transition to everyday life." I pointed to the second shot. "That one is for Megan. She's twenty-five and was arrested for street racing. I don't know her whole story, but she swears she was running from her abusive boyfriend who was trying to run her off the road. She hasn't talked much about it, but I'm sure she has her reasons. She doesn't mind jail because she feels safer there."

The bartender set a plate in front of each of us. The burgers were enormous, and next to them were piles of fries and onion rings. I pulled a crisp fry from the plate and placed it in my mouth. A soft murmur of ecstasy escaped.

Kerrick's eyes lit up. He seemed to gain something from giving me a small piece of pleasure. My tongue slipped past my lips to the cheeseburger I now held in my hand. Mayonnaise caught at the corner of my mouth. I circled my lips and snatched up the creamy white dot. He shifted several times in his seat. *Interesting.*

Shaking his head, he picked up his burger and dug in. Conversation halted as we both lost ourselves in the meal.

Picking up the third shot, Kerrick asked about the girl behind the drink.

"This one belongs to Natalie. She's completely guilty of her crime. She likes expensive things. One night, she found a watch in the washroom—a watch she convinced herself should be hers. She pocketed it instead of returning it. She knew she should have given it back, but she didn't. She forgot Cartier put serial numbers on their merchandise. The police found the forty-thousand-dollar watch in her eight-hundred-dollar-a-month apartment. The sheer value of the item sent her to prison for three years. I think she became a huge fan of Timex from that point on."

He laughed at the stories I told. Sipping his soda, he held up the fourth shot and tilted his head in question.

"That one's in honor of Robyn. She's a martial art instructor and was solely responsible for me not being raped in prison. She taught me how to defend myself from day one. If you're not shirking off the advances of the guards, then you're trying to keep the lonely woman from trying to settle between your legs. She's there because she put a thief in the hospital after he tried to steal her purse. She's doing time because as a fourth-degree black belt, she was considered a deadly weapon. They said she used excessive force with him. She's been there the longest and has about eight months left to her sentence."

"Well, here's to the girls," he said as he slid the drinks one by one in front of me. Wrapped in a napkin were several slices of lime he placed next to the salt shaker and the shot glasses.

I took the four glasses and tossed them back one after another. Shivers ran down my spine as the liquor warmed my body from the inside out. When I got to the last glass, I held it high and said, "The fifth one is for me. I did a year in prison because I'd had enough of Morgan. He did some awful stuff to me. The last straw was when he decided to fuck a girl on the hood of his car in front of my house. He had just beaten me to a pulp, and I knifed his tires and a little more. Unfortunately, they were expensive tires, and I left a mark on his pretty little face. That sent me away for twelve months."

I took a lime for the first time tonight, licked my hand, salted it, licked it again, tossed back the shot, and sucked on the lime. I squirmed in my seat, reacting to the mixture.

"That seems excessive for the crime. It was tires, for God's sake. You didn't stab the man, did you?" He grabbed the empty glasses one by one and stacked them in a tower between us.

"No, I whacked him upside the head, but I wanted to stab him."

"What did you learn from the experience?"

"I learned if you're going to knife someone's tires, then you should probably make sure the owner isn't watching you while he's screwing some blonde on the hood, and when you take a swing with a tire iron, you should aim for the little head between his legs, not the big fat one on his shoulders. At lastly, make sure you don't wave the knife at his dick as he chases you around the car. Men are very protective of their junk."

Chapter 3

KERRICK

My laughter caused several people to look our way. It had been a long time since I'd doubled up like that. I was enjoying my time with Mickey, and that surprised me. Her eyes followed mine to the dance floor. She had a look of longing while she watched people sway to the music.

"Let's dance." I hopped off the stool and pulled her with me. She tottered on her heels before catching her balance and following me to the center of the room. Maneuvering through the throng of people, we situated ourselves in the middle of the dance floor just as the next song began to play.

"I don't know any of this music," she complained. She moved her body to the distinctive beat of the song.

"Just listen to the pulse, it's like any music. Feel the beat and move." With my hands on her hips, I directed her body in rhythm with mine. She might be skinny, but boy, could she move. I wasn't sure what attracted me, but I felt the pull from her the minute I'd seen her. Even plain faced and dressed in baggy jeans, she was hot.

She closed her eyes and got lost in the beat of her music. My hands slid up her back, and I pulled her against my chest possessively. She felt perfect in my arms. I'd have sworn we'd danced this way thousands of times. The stiffness that had been present melted away as she relaxed against me.

Her life had changed drastically in twenty-four hours. Prison. Freedom. Abandonment. Destitution. She needed protection, and I vowed to watch her like a hawk. She was my singular focus. Her head fell back, showing her long, slender neck. I tightened my hold as the music took on a slower, sensual pace.

Her head fell forward against my chest and tucked perfectly under my chin. I leaned down and inhaled the scent of her hair. Three minutes of pure bliss was all I got before the music changed.

"What song is this?" Her blue eyes lifted in question. She breathed deeply, burying her nose in my shirt.

"It's called 'Chandelier'. Listen to the lyrics, it's perfect for you. Tonight you can swing from the chandeliers. Just hold on, I'll make sure no one bothers you."

"What if I want to be bothered? It's been so long since I've been in a man's arms—in a man's bed."

"You're in my arms tonight. You can drink until you puke and dance until you drop, but I won't let a strange man take you anywhere. You need to take baby steps, Mickey." I guided her off the dance floor and back to the table. With a firm hold on her waist, I lifted her onto the stool and told her to stay put.

"Cockblocker," she yelled as I walked toward the bar. My shoulders shook with laughter. She was a tiny, sexy dynamo who smelled fucking amazing. I hadn't wanted to let her go since I'd led her to the dance floor. She tested every gallant bone in my body.

With a soda, a glass of water, and two more shots of tequila, I returned to find her chair empty. *Damn her. She was told to stay put.* I wound my way through the crowd. Eyes trained to look for detail searched the dance floor. Smack dab in the center, she was dancing with another man. Tension ran from my clenched jaw to my balled fists. I had no claim to her, but I'd be damned if she was hooking up with someone while she was under my watch.

What the hell did she think she was doing? She was drunk and was acting irresponsibly. I walked to the center of the dance floor, took her arm and pulled her toward the edge.

"Dude, get your own date. She's mine," the stranger said in a Larry the Cable Guy voice.

"Fuck off, buddy. She came with me, and she'll leave with me." I flashed my badge at the man coming toward me. He retreated. Nothing stops a bully like a police badge.

With my hand on her back, I moved her toward the table. "I told you not to move. You're drunk, and men are assholes. That's a bad combination. Stick close to me, so you don't get hurt."

"You're a man. What makes you better than the rest? Who's going to protect me from you?" Her soft blue eyes penetrated my hard outer shell. They sought an answer I couldn't give her—an honest one. I wasn't better than the rest. In fact, I could be the worst possible scenario for her. On the other hand, maybe we were both what the other needed. It was something to consider.

"You don't need protection from me. I'm here to take care of you." *Was I trying to convince her or me?*

"I'm fine. I know the guy, and so he's not exactly a stranger." One after the other, she tossed back the shots I'd brought, not bothering with the lime this time. When her head leaned back to get the last drop, she lost her balance and near fell off the stool. With the grace and speed of a ninja, I plucked her off the chair and sat her back down.

"Thanks for the save. Let me get you a drink. What are you drinking?" The words slurred together and sounded more like— wahr you dreaning?

"Diet soda, and I've drunk too much of it." I eyed her with skepticism. "I have to piss, Mickey. Don't leave this seat." I was hesitant to leave her, but I had to go bad.

"Go pee, Detective. I'll be fine." She leaned her head on the table and stared at the dance floor.

"Don't go anywhere with anyone. I mean it, Mickey." I all but ran to the john. *What the fuck did I get myself into?*

I was gone a few minutes, only to return and find her missing. Again. *Shit.* She was back on the dance floor with some jackass, who was basically dry humping her in the middle of the floor. Dancing with her back to him, she appeared to be in a world of her own and oblivious to his actions, but I wasn't. I wanted to put my fist through the man's mouth.

It was time to prove my point. Men were assholes and maybe having some guy go too far might scare her into obedience. I itched to kick some ass, but I took the wait-and-see approach and stood against the back wall.

The man danced up on her, grinding against her back end. She swatted at him. He turned her around, yanked her to his chest and tried to kiss her. She stomped on his instep and pushed against his chest with all her might. Stumbling backward, the man fell into a crowd of partiers.

A big man pulled the hobbled man from the floor and tossed him against the wall. That's when all hell broke loose. It took three large steps to get to Mickey and remove her from the melee. *So much for the wait-and-see approach.*

Not wanting to be a recipient of her back-alley self-defense techniques, I tossed her over my shoulder and removed her from the dance floor. Once the bar tab was settled, we were out of the building.

"Put me down. What do you think you're doing?" The sharp slice of her shriek cut through the thick night air. "I want to dance! Put me down." She wiggled her too-skinny ass, but I had her pinned and she wasn't going anywhere unless I allowed it.

"Your fun ended when you started a brawl. I told you to stay. But no…you had to go and start a fight. By the way, where did you learn that move?" I tossed her forward and steadied her as her feet touched the ground. She stumbled forward into my chest. Even in four-inch heels, she barely came to my chin. Lifting her face to look at me, the robin-egg blue of her eyes left me speechless. I was in serious trouble. I knew I was exactly what she didn't need, but I'd be damned if I could stop myself from investigating the possibilities. Her lips puckered with each word as she answered my question. Her plump, rosy red lips called to me.

"Robyn taught me a few things. Prison is dangerous. One of the night guards cornered me once and copped a feel. I vowed then to learn how to protect myself."

The thought of a stranger's hands taking liberties with her body pissed me off. "Tonight, I'll protect you. There's no need for you to unman a stranger in the bar. This wouldn't have happened if you had behaved and stayed where I told you to stay." My eyes never left her lips.

"He was no stranger. We went to prom together, and if you plan to hang around me, you should get used to the fact that I rarely behave."

Feeling an incredible urge to conquer her, I crushed my lips against hers. I felt her brief hesitation seconds before she rose up and took what I offered.

Soft kisses and swaying hips coaxed me to dive deeper and probe harder. She let out a sexy whimper when she pressed into my growing hardness.

I had to make an immediate decision. If I continued to kiss her, there was no doubt where this night would end. If I pulled away, everything would go back to normal.

With the majority of blood pooling in my pants, I was grateful for the remnants left in my brain.

It was difficult, but I pulled away and pushed her body toward the truck.

"Why'd you stop?" she purred. "I like your kisses, and I want more of them." She nuzzled into my neck. *This woman was trouble with a capital T.*

"I like your kisses, too, but I'm supposed to be protecting you against lechers. I'm not supposed to be the lecher. You're drunk. Let's see if you want to kiss me tomorrow when you're sober."

"I do. I will. I wanted to kiss you today while I was looking at your scruff in the car. You have no idea what I was thinking about then, but it was really naughty." She bit her lip like she was trying to stop the words from escaping.

I leaned her unsteady body up against the side panel of my truck and opened the door.

"I just wanted to have a good time. Stop being such a killjoy. Do you even know how to have fun?" With my hands on her hips, I lifted her into the front seat and proceeded to buckle her up. She smelled like a walking distillery, but once you got past the tequila, she smelled of sweetened coconut and mango.

"I know how to have fun. I just want to make sure you're sober and in your right mind when we decide to play. You need to adapt to your life before you add in other distractions."

"You stopped kissing me because I have a skinny ass, and you're not attracted to me."

I laughed at the ridiculousness of her statement. If she only knew what was running through my head when I held her, she would retract that immediately.

"You're an asshole, Kerrick. Take me home, I'm not feeling well."

I shut her door and rushed to the driver's seat. "Don't you dare puke in my car."

"It would serve you right for laughing at me." She collapsed against the window, leaning her head on the cool glass. I hoped the temperature offered relief to her queasy stomach. I didn't do barf.

"I'm warning you, Mickey, if you feel sick, you better tell me right away. I don't do throw up." I shoved the truck in gear and drove, all the while watching her out of the corner of my eye. Even sulking she was beautiful, but not in a conventional sort of way. Her hair was unruly, and her legs were too long, but it was her eyes that hypnotized me.

Ten minutes later, I helped her from the truck and directed her into the house. She handed me the keys and leaned heavily against the door while I unlocked it. I walked her to the living room and sat her on the couch. She would be feeling this tomorrow.

In search of water and some type of painkiller, I found both in the kitchen. When I returned, she was sprawled on the couch, fast asleep, looking peaceful and carefree. In her slumber, she didn't have to think about the tough hurdles coming her way.

This was supposed to be a cattle ranch, and yet I hadn't seen or smelled any evidence leading me to believe there were any cows in the vicinity.

The condition of the land suggested no one had been here to oversee the property. She definitely had a lot to deal with. I took a walk through the house and found her room. It was the only one with a feminine touch and dresses in the closet.

I scooped her into my arms. For a full-grown woman, she was light and in need of fattening up. I liked my women curvier. The fact that I was thinking of her as mine should have caused me concern, but at this moment all I wanted to do was make sure she was okay. Settled on her bed, I tucked her in for the night.

She turned to her side and snuggled the pillow. A pang of jealousy washed over me. How I wished I were her pillow.

My lips pressed against the top of her head before I slipped quietly from her room. There was no way I was leaving her drunk and alone. Settled on the couch for the night, I made myself as comfortable as a six-foot-four-inch man could be on a five-foot sofa.

SHE'D NEED a hearty breakfast this morning. Plates I'd filled with bacon and eggs were placed on the table before I went to wake her. She might be okay weighing less than a bale of hay, but I knew if she were going to run the ranch, she needed to be in top form. Her baggy clothes nearly fell from her body, which told me she was far from being herself.

I stood nearby while she slept. Curly brown locks fell across the pillow. The bow of her lip puckered with each exhale. A soft, puffing noise escaped with each breath. It was a sign of how exhausted she was. I doubted she'd had a good night's sleep in the last year.

I felt bad for having to wake her this early, but she needed to dive back into her life, a life that by all appearances had disappeared while she was away.

With a gentle push on her shoulder, I nudged her. I considered kissing her awake, but I didn't want to end up like the idiot on the dance floor. Kissing her awake would have been more fun, but being able to walk seemed practical.

If last night's kiss was any evidence of her pent-up passion, I wanted a repeat. However, neither one of us needed the complications at this point in our lives. Sleeping through my first nudge, I shook her a second time with more zeal.

She bolted from the bed with her fists in the air. The dress she'd slept in was bunched around her waist, her pink lace underwear in full view. Hair floated in front of her face and entered her mouth. *Thoop, thoop, thoop,* she tried to spit it to the side, but the moisture from her tongue acted like glue. One hand flailed in front of her face, desperately trying to get it under control.

"What the hell, Kerrick? What are you doing here?" She relaxed her posture and pulled the dress down as far as she could. She glanced slowly between the bed and me. She had an accusatory expression that insinuated I'd been less than a gentleman.

"I slept on the couch. I couldn't in good conscience leave you drunk and alone." She looked no worse for the wear. However, she had to have some residual effects from drinking so much last night. "How are you feeling?" If it were me, I'd be lying with my face near the toilet. I was surprised she hadn't needed to pray to the porcelain gods.

"Like I was hit by your truck." She grabbed her head and fell prone on the bed.

"I made you breakfast. Get up."

"No, I just want to sleep. Besides, I'm not a big fan of Pop-Tarts," she said with sarcasm while she pulled the covers up and around her neck. "Stop trying to fatten me up." She covered her face with the blanket and rolled away from me.

"No, smart ass, I made you bacon and eggs. There's also fresh coffee. Get your too-skinny ass out of bed and come eat." I turned and walked out of the room.

Several minutes later, she emerged, wearing a pair of Mickey Mouse shorts and a red T-shirt. Covering her feet were the well-worn cowboy boots she'd had on yesterday. The outfit would look ridiculous on anyone else, but on her it was hot. *Get it together, Kerrick.*

"What time is it?" The heel of her palm rubbed at her eyes.

"It's six-thirty."

"What the hell, Kerrick? I'm out of prison. I was hoping to sleep all morning."

"You did sleep all morning. I was going to get you up an hour ago, but I thought you might want to sleep in." I tossed a piece of cold toast on her plate. "Didn't they wake you at five for breakfast?" I pushed a glass of water and two painkillers toward her. "Eat the toast first, then take these. I can tell by the squint of your eyes you're not feeling well."

"Good observation, but it doesn't take a detective to see I'm hungover. The black rings under my eyes would have been your first clue, and just for the record, breakfast is served at five-thirty." She picked up her fork and took a small bite of scrambled egg. Her eyes rolled back in their sockets, and a moan of pure pleasure escaped her mouth. *So, she was vocal when she found pleasure.* I thought about the many things I could do to make her moan.

"You got to sleep an extra hour." Everything about her intrigued me. I saw a strong-willed woman who had the system strip her of her dignity and confidence. I'd watched her walk out of prison yesterday. The first steps were uncertain, but the farther she got away from the prison, the more confident her gait became.

She'd attacked the burden of putting her house back together with the determination of a toothless man committed to eating a steak. She seemed like she'd just keep chewing off bit by bit until she had consumed what she needed to survive. Picking up a piece of bacon, I took a bite and waited for her response.

"Is there something I'm missing here? Have you been assigned to me as some kind of new integration program counselor?" She slathered her toast with enough strawberry jam to cause a diabetic coma. "I opted to serve my entire sentence so I didn't have a parole officer."

I wanted to laugh. She served her entire sentence because she had to. You didn't get a parole office after a year stint in the pen.

Her indignant attitude amused me. Laughter bubbled while I digested her comeback. "No, I've assigned myself to you. It just goes to show, you shouldn't get into a car with a stranger. You never know what you're going to get yourself into. Now eat your breakfast. I believe you have a ranch to inspect."

With feigned exasperation, Mickey rolled her eyes.

"I want to see your badge or something to prove you are who you say you are. You told me you were a detective, but I haven't seen anything to support that statement."

"It's a bit late to check my credentials, don't you think? I've been in your house all night. You really should be less trusting. I could be a serial killer or a nice guy, but you wouldn't know."

"Which are you?" She picked up our empty plates and deposited them in the sink. Walking back to the table, she raised her coffee cup and swallowed the remaining contents in one gulp.

"Neither." I pulled my wallet out of my back pocket and showed her the same badge I'd flashed last night. Sliding my business card from the side pocket, I placed it on the table in front of her. She eyed it with uncertainty before she picked it up. After scanning the card, she tossed it back on the table.

"Seems like you're the real deal."

"I'm definitely the real deal. Do you want to change your clothes before we head out? Shorts, although they show off your lovely legs, are probably not ideal for traversing several thousand acres."

She opened her mouth like I'd said something shocking.

"How do you know the size of my ranch?" Her hands rested on her hips in a defiant manner. One hip jutted out as if to say, *Don't lie to me*.

"I'm a detective, Sugar, and a good one at that. You have about thirty seconds before we leave."

"Have you forgotten this property belongs to me?" She backed away, looking over her shoulder. God, she was beautiful.

"Nope. Have you?" I pushed the chair back and headed to the front door. I felt her eyes on me as I exited. The thought of her watching me made my dick twitch. I readjusted my hard-on as soon as I exited the house.

Five minutes later, she emerged dressed in blue jeans, a red T-shirt, and boots. Her hair was tamed and pulled into a ponytail.

"Where shall we start?" I asked, but I was already walking toward the stables. That was where I wanted to start.

"By all means, Detective, lead the way. Maybe you can tell me where my cattle are? Have you seen a cow anywhere? What about a ranch hand? I had four of them when I left."

"You had four cows or four ranch hands? If it's four cattle, I couldn't with a straight face call you a rancher."

She ran to catch up. "Ranch hands, asshole. Are you always this difficult? I bet you're a real treat to date, or are you married? If so, did she throw you out, and that's why I'm somehow stuck with you?"

Wow, she was so close to the truth, and yet so far off the mark. I didn't like the way she managed to find my weak spots. "Don't worry, I'll grow on you."

"Yeah, like mold. You didn't answer the wife question. By your omission, you must have one. Does she know where you were last night?" She raised her eyebrows and pressed for an answer.

"I don't have a wife, and I'm not looking for one." The brusqueness of my voice seemed to make her retreat. She backed away from me, and I made a note to myself to look into that behavior. She bantered like a pro, but the minute a voice was raised, she cowered and retreated. *Shit, scaring her wasn't my intention.*

"Sorry, it was none of my business," she whispered meekly.

"You can ask. I'm just sensitive about the marriage topic. My mom badgers me about marriage all the time. You would think her grandparent biological clock was ticking. It's not like she doesn't have other options. I have four siblings, but for some reason, she's set her sights on me. Again."

She closed the distance between us.

"It's because she loves you, and she doesn't want to see you die a single, disagreeable old man. You have the disagreeable part down pat—it's probably just a character flaw, and so it's unlikely you'll change—but single is something you can control." There was a sparkle in her eyes as she razzed me. I was glad she had segued from fear to funny in a breath.

"I'll show you disagreeable." I leaned over and picked her up. Throwing her over my shoulder, I carried her to the stables. All the while, she beat on my back and yelled for me to put her down. I could hardly make out the words she screamed, because they were laced with laughter and profanities that could make a sailor blush. It was good to hear her laugh.

At the door to the stables, I flipped her over like a sack of cement and set her on her feet.

"Why are you always throwing me over your shoulder? I can walk just fine, you know."

I pinched her chin between my thumb and forefinger and made her look directly at me. "I like putting you over my shoulder. Be thankful I haven't put you over my knee." At her gasp, I busted a hearty laugh.

"Shhh, you're too loud. I have a headache." She held her head like it was at risk of falling apart. Of course, her screaming was acceptable. My laughter frowned upon. *Women.*

"Seven shots within two hours will do that to a person. Let it be a lesson to you. The only reason you didn't get sick was that I insisted you eat first." My look challenged her to disagree. "By the way, you gave me way too much money. I put your change on the table."

She said something about not wanting to owe me anything. "Is it your self-appointed job to be my babysitter? If so, you're fired."

"You can't fire me. Hell, you can't hire me because you can't afford me. Let's go inside." I pulled her hand toward the door. Her eyes fell, and her body stiffened.

She inhaled deeply, squared her shoulders and moved timidly forward. It didn't take a detective to see something about the stables didn't sit right with her.

Chapter 4

MICKEY

In my head, I heard Holly recite Mark Burnett's quote, "Facing your fears robs them of their power." My heart felt heavy the minute I stepped inside. With a flip of a switch, the fluorescent bulb buzzed to life and the dim space became light. The room held my greatest joys and worst heartaches.

"It looks like someone stole your horses, too." Kerrick walked ahead of me and peeked into the stalls. "How many did you have? By the looks of it, you could house at least twenty."

"Twenty-two, but I had twelve." I walked to where he stood in the door of the dusty tack room. At the far end of the space were rows of tack stands covered in tarps. With a yank, he pulled the sheeting from one. Dust billowed in the air and slowly floated to the floor.

A slow whistle sounded from his mouth. Of all the saddles he could have unearthed, he uncovered the one that had the potential to cause the most pain. After two years under that dusty tarp, the leather had a just-polished patina. It was exactly the same as the day I'd removed it from Mr. Darcy for the last time.

"This was your saddle." It was a statement, not a question. His hand caressed the saddle like a man caressed his lover.

"Yep." I nodded my head and moved to cover it back up. Before I could throw the cover back over it, he pulled the tarp from my hands and tossed it in the corner.

"This saddle cost a fortune, it's a custom job and says a lot about the rider. The detail to the fenders is incredible." He slid his fingers across the finely worked leather. "This is a show saddle, and a fine one at that. The hand-tooled flowers show intricate detail." He traced the prickly thistle in the center. "What's the symbolism of the flower and the thistle? It's an odd combination." His hand cupped the horn and slid across the seat to rub the cantle.

"My dad used to tell me I was as pretty as a flower and as prickly as a thorn." Conflicting emotions roiled inside me. I struggled to breathe. Regret sucked the oxygen from the air. Guilt pressed the remaining molecules from my lungs. Tears pooled in the corners of my eyes.

Swiping at the first tear that fell, I turned and ran from the room. The blood that pounded in my ears muffled all sound. Once outside, I grabbed my head and sank to my knees. My emotional dam had finally collapsed. I sensed his presence before I heard him. Strong arms reached under me and cradled my body. In one swift movement, I was in his arms and moving away from the stables.

"I'm fine. Put me down." When I squirmed, he released me. Robyn's voice echoed in my head, reminding me that showing vulnerability made me appear weak. I couldn't afford to be weak. I was determined to be strong. Stronger.

"What was that all about?" He stood in front of me, cupping my head in his palms while he brushed the tears from my face with his thumbs. "Please tell me."

I swallowed the lump in my throat. "It's just a lot to take in. I haven't been here for a year, and so much has changed." Quickly patching the hole in my internal floodgate, I pulled from his touch and headed for the barn.

"I understand." He walked beside me and reached down to grab my hand. His fingers weaved between mine while he redirected my thoughts with a question.

Set Free

"What's in the barn?" We approached the unlocked door. Dropping my hand, Kerrick pulled on the wooden panels and listened to the rusty hinges complain about the intrusion.

"An ATV, I hope. Since all the tack is still here, that's a good sign the ranch hasn't been stripped bare."

The smell of stale air assailed me upon entering the damp enclosure. I tossed the switch, and the bare bulb flickered to life. In the center of the barn sat the beat-up ATV. It was like seeing an old friend.

Opening the gas cap, I shook the vehicle and listened for the slosh of liquid. Feeling satisfied there was enough fuel to get us where we needed to go, I hopped on the seat, turned the key and pressed the ignition button. The engine grumbled but died. I tried again and got the same result. Frustrated, I banged my fist on the tank and hung my head in defeat.

"Let me try," he said, lifting me from the seat. He took my place, and with a single try the engine roared to life.

"Don't get smug, Detective. I primed it for you," I yelled over the rumble of the engine.

"Get on, Sugar. I'll take you for a ride." He patted the seat behind him.

I gave him a dirty look and climbed on the vehicle. Why did I follow his lead without question?

With my hands wrapped around his waist, I held on for dear life. After a few lurching movements, he propelled the ATV steadily forward.

Pointing toward the opening in the fence, I guided him through my property. The land was vast but overgrown, so we followed the fence line. It was obvious cattle had been absent for months, maybe longer. The grass was tall and dense. The feed bins were matted down and resembled hardtack. The natural ponds dotting the landscape were healthy and full.

Wildflowers littered the landscape, creating a soft foreground in contrast to the rugged hills that lay beyond.

Several hours later, I guided him to a fenced-in area. He killed the engine, leaving us in silence. I climbed off the vehicle and walked to where the iron gate stood ajar.

"Where are we?" He slid off the ATV and joined me. His eyes scanned the area, and a glimmer of recognition crossed his face.

"The cemetery. I figured I should visit my dad and apologize for completely fucking everything up."

"Mickey, it's going to be all right. You'll figure it out." He tried to rub my shoulders, but I shook free of him and headed into the small space, leaving him behind.

Standing in front of my father's gravestone, I wept.

"I'm sorry, Daddy. I totally messed everything up. I had to go away for a year, and it looks like I lost everything you worked so hard for." I sank to my knees and pulled the weeds that had grown in my absence.

"I seem to always let you down. I should have been there the day you died, but I failed you then, and I'm failing you now. I'm so sorry." Gut-wrenching, lung-searing sobs wracked my body.

I cleared out my sorrow weed by weed. Handfuls of grass flew through the air, and I exorcised my demons.

In the distance, I heard a cough and turned to find Kerrick leaning against the wrought iron gate. His forehead creased with concern.

I didn't want his pity or his concerned looks. I wanted to be left alone to grieve and sort through my anger. Embarrassed by my tears, I wiped them away and addressed his presence.

"You don't need to be here. This is my job, and mine alone."

"Mickey, you're not alone. I'm not leaving." He strode toward the grave I was working on.

"I need to finish cleaning off my grandparents' graves. You could be here for a while."

"My schedule is fluid. I work my cases as they come, and it's been fairly quiet lately. I'll help you." He leaned down and pulled the weeds beside me. We worked in tandem to clear up the unkempt plot of land. I plucked the last dandelion from Adelaide Mercer's grave. A feeling of accomplishment settled over me as I rose from the dirt. Covered in mud, I felt cleansed.

"Are you ready to leave?" Wiping the dirt from my knees, I walked out the gate, climbed onto the back of the ATV and waited for Kerrick to join me.

The sense of safety and calm I'd felt when I left prison was an illusion. I left knowing I had money, a steady income, and a house. In reality, there was a very good chance I had nothing. In the best possible light, I was hanging by a thread.

Hugging tight to the only thing that seemed real, I grasped Kerrick around the waist and squeezed. His hand rested on mine as he drove us over the hill and back into the barn. With my head lying against his back, I held on a bit longer than I should have. We sat on the silent vehicle in the middle of the barn. He made no attempt to dislodge me. It was as if he understood my need to connect.

Reluctantly, I released my hold on him and slid from the seat. Feeling beaten and broken, I walked to the open door.

"Wait up. Are you okay?" He rushed to my side and shifted my head up, as if the angle would give him insight into my thoughts. The tenderness in his eyes caught my breath. They never strayed from mine. They sought and searched.

"No, I feel empty. This ranch has been in my family for over a century. My ancestors are buried here, and it was my job to make sure they could rest in peace. How peaceful will it be for them when another family owns their land? Who will clean their graves and plant flowers for them? I don't know what I'm going to do." Feeling ashamed, I tried to hide my tear-streaked cheeks, but Kerrick wouldn't let me escape.

"You're down, but you're not out." He released my chin and turned back to shut the barn door. "Let's go inside and figure out a plan. Look at the assets you have, and put them to work for you." This stranger who knew nothing about me seemed to understand me anyway.

"I must look pathetic to you." He seemed to measure my words. "You should turn and run in the other direction." Maybe he had already considered it.

"Mickey, you're not pathetic, you're overwhelmed." He slung his arm over my shoulders and gave me the squeeze of courage I desperately needed. "It looks like a mess when you look at the big picture, so you need to break it down."

"Even broken down, it's a lot to deal with."

"Where in the hell is your support system? Who are the people who were supposed to have your back?"

In a voice that belied my true feelings, I tried to convince us both that things would be okay.

"I shouldn't complain. I have a ranch, a house, an amazing stable, an arena, eight newly refinished cabins, a barn, and thousands of acres of land." I turned and pointed as I rattled off the assets. "The problem is, no matter what I do, I can't replace the cattle that are no longer here. I have no ranch hands, and no money to hire any." A cloud passed in front of the sun, casting gloom on the day. "I have a property in need of maintenance and a home equity loan that needs to be paid. I've lived my entire life with men who ran everything, and they've all abandoned me."

It was interesting how the people I was raised by had disappeared, but a stranger was willing to step in and take their place. *What about loyalty?* Sure, I'd screwed everything up, but where were the men who had promised to remain loyal to my father and his memory? Surprised? Not really. The men in my life had been less than dependable and never predictable.

"Go to the bank and figure out what's happened there." He spoke with authority. "When you get home, write out your plan. You can do this." He sounded so convincing, I almost believed him.

"I don't know how to attack this, Kerrick. My dad took care of things my whole life. When he died, everything kind of ran itself. Or so I thought." I was facing a less-than-perfect situation, and it shamed me. "I was blind to what was happening. I trusted Morgan to keep it all under control. He has a vested interest in the success of the property. Where in the hell did he go, and what did he do with all of our assets?"

"Would you like me to find him? It's what I do." His eyes searched mine for an answer.

"I don't know what to do or what I want." I envied the ostrich that buried their heads in the sand. All I wanted to do right now was climb into bed and cover my head. "Maybe it will all go away." Morgan was the biggest mistake I'd never make again.

"It won't go away, but neither will I." Shaking his head, he pulled me to his chest. "I'll help you see this through. I can't solve it for you, but I'm happy to assist you in whatever you need." My head fit perfectly under his chin. "You have to do this on your own to realize how capable you are." I wrapped my arms around his waist and exhaled. In that moment, that was where I wanted to be. "Go to the bank, Mickey, so you can figure out your next move."

It had been a long time since any man had thought me capable. Surprisingly, my father left twenty percent of the family legacy to a relative stranger. Maybe it was his way of making sure someone he thought competent had some control. Even Daddy got it wrong.

With my head against his chest, I relaxed for a moment before I had to let go and move forward. That one moment may have been the best part of my day. But I needed more. More affection. Just more. Didn't he promise to kiss me if I wanted it when I was sober? Let's see if he was more talk than action.

"Last night, you told me you would kiss me if I wanted it. I'm sober, and I want you to kiss me." I pulled back and waited for his reaction. Would it be one of annoyance or repulsion to my weakness? "Are you a man of your word, Detective McKinley?"

His beautiful brown eyes darkened with a look of passion and hunger. Could it be possible Kerrick McKinley liked me? If so, I felt grateful for his lack of good judgment.

Soft lips brushed lightly against mine. Strong hands embraced my body, one pulling me toward him, and the other wrapping around my hair. His control of my body was complete. I couldn't move from his embrace if I tried—if I wanted to. I wanted him to take control of something, and if it was just a kiss, then so be it.

His soft kiss turned into something more—something fierce but undefined. He nibbled on my lower lip. I melted into his embrace. He no longer needed to hold me there. It wasn't like I'd run away. Wasn't this what I was craving? Wasn't this the precursor to priority number one? When I let out a moan, he slid his tongue along my bottom lip and into my mouth. With precision, he explored the hot, moist recesses, spending extra time softly caressing my tongue. Weak in the knees, I dipped toward the ground, only to be lifted to his waist. His hands had switched positions and now sat firmly beneath my ass. With my arms around his neck, I lifted my legs around his waist and we moved in the direction of the house. My fervent hope was that he took me straight to bed.

Placed gently on top of the bedspread, his body pressed me deep into the pillow-top mattress. The hard outline of his arousal pushed against my hip. This was exactly what I wanted.

"Have sex with me, Kerrick," my choppy voice begged. "I want to feel something good. I want to connect with something real." Reaching between our bodies, I tugged at his belt buckle. He groaned before he reached down to stop my progress.

"No." He rolled off me and lay next to me on the bed. "We're not doing this." He spoke to me like an errant child.

My passion was replaced by a sense of loss.

"Why the hell not?" Frustrated because he had once again set me aside, I rolled away. The last thing I wanted him to see was the hurt I felt from his rejection.

"Mickey, it shouldn't happen this way. You're the kind of girl who should have a boyfriend, not a quick fuck." The way he said the word 'fuck' made it sound so dirty.

"You seem to be quite the expert on me. Contrary to your belief, what I need is to get laid, so I can be done with it and move on. I've done the boyfriend thing, and it hasn't worked out for me. Just be honest, you're not interested. That's easier for me to take than some lie you've devised to lessen the pain of rejection."

Pulling me over, he grabbed my hand and placed it on his bulging erection. "This is how uninterested and unaffected I am." I palmed the length of him before I pulled it back in surprise. "I haven't wanted someone as much as you in a long time, but not under these circumstances. Besides, what I want to do to you would take a very long time."

My heart beat fast, and my breath grew shallow at his words.

What could he want to do to me that would take longer than twenty minutes?

He glanced at his watch. "Don't you have a meeting at the bank in twenty minutes?"

"Oh shit," I hollered, flying from the bed. I left him laughing while I raced to ready myself for the meeting. Disappearing into my closet, I changed my clothes and grabbed the money I'd need to settle up with the bank. I emerged wearing a sundress and sandals. Running my fingers through my hair, I tried to tame the curls floating around my face.

Leaning on his elbow, he was a delicious confection laid out on my bed. "Do you want to go out to dinner?"

"I'm eating at home tonight. I have two great pieces of salmon to cook." I walked into the connecting bathroom to splash water on my tear-stained face.

"I like salmon," he called from the room. "Are you inviting me to dinner, or are you kindly telling me you're not interested?" He sat up and moved to the edge of the bed.

Walking to him with purpose, I grabbed his hand and placed it under my dress and between my legs. Rubbing his fingers across my drenched underwear, his eyes widened before I released my grip on him.

"That's how uninterested I am. See you at six." Turning around, I walked quickly out the door.

I walked out the front door and prayed my truck would start.

It was hard to shock a confident man like Kerrick. Obviously, the prison had some lasting effects on me, one being the total disintegration of my moral compass.

Climbing into my truck, I inserted the key into the ignition and turned it. The engine roared to life on the first try. *Thank you, God.* Backing out of the driveway, I turned the truck around and headed into town. Kerrick was leaning against the doorjamb, his *I'll get you back* expression fading in my rearview mirror as I drove away. *Yep, I still had it.* My confidence climbed a notch knowing I was able to affect him.

I hadn't asked him to be a part of my life, and I wasn't sure how he'd so quickly integrated himself into it. Did I want to have sex with him? Hell, yes. But was that all I wanted? I didn't particularly like him taking charge, and yet I did. Would he back away after we slept together? Time would tell.

Chapter 5

MICKEY

"I have an appointment to see April Donovan. My name is Michelle Mercer." The young girl at the counter glanced at me, then back at her computer. Picking up her phone, she pressed in three numbers and spoke.

"Ms. Donovan, Michelle Mercer is here to see you."

Within minutes, a middle-aged brunette walked toward the front of the bank and introduced herself as April Donovan before she escorted me to a side office.

I sat in a chair made for looks rather than comfort and waited for her to begin. It felt like a trip to the principal's office. I'd only been there once, but it wasn't a visit I was likely to forget. Nor was the sharp sting of my daddy's belt across my butt when he found out I'd cut class to go shopping with some girls. I had wanted to know what it would feel like to hang around other females. I wasn't afforded that opportunity living on the ranch.

"Did you hear me, Ms. Mercer?"

"Oh no, sorry. Can you repeat what you said?" *Focus, Mercer*, I told myself. This was important stuff.

"I asked if you brought the money to bring your account to good standing?"

"Yes, of course. I brought the money, as well as additional funds. I want to close the existing account and open a new one."

Ms. Donovan went straight to work the minute I placed the cash on the table. She counted the bills one by one. She had the dexterity of a Vegas dealer, or possibly a magician. I'd never seen a person shuffle through cash that fast. I halfway expected a puff of smoke to erupt—and poof, it would all disappear.

"I have printed out all the paperwork you requested. It looks like the biggest outlying expenses from your account come from a ranching supply store in Lone Tree."

No surprise there. It was one of Morgan's favorite places to shop. I wondered what was purchased the last year while I was gone.

"Thank you. I'll be stopping by there on my way home."

We raced through the remaining paperwork. Thirty minutes later, I exited with lighter pockets and a heavier heart. Things were so much worse than I'd expected.

At the ranching supply store, I was told I had outfitted my foreman with the finest boots, hats, and clothes available. I might no longer have cattle, but I had the best-dressed foreman around town.

Another little tidbit of information that came my way was Morgan had been purchasing roping saddles and miscellaneous gear for rodeo competitions within the last month. Morgan had bragged to anyone who would listen about his busy summer on the rodeo circuit. That would explain his absence and embezzlement of funds. I canceled the existing account and set up new parameters for future purchases before I left.

My last stop before home was the cell phone store to reactivate my account. With a new connection to the world, I felt ready to conquer the world—or at least another bowl of ice cream.

To my astonishment, the grass in front of my house had been cut. I inhaled the sweet smell of clipping. Someone had made quick work of cleaning up the place. A feeling of joy floated over me. Maybe I wasn't alone after all. With renewed energy and a sense of purpose, I set out to find the ranch hands that had finally stepped up to their given tasks.

I listened for signs of life coming from any direction but was greeted by silence. Were they out in the fields? Maybe they were behind the cabins, in the stables built for the help?

Approaching cabin eight, I peeked in the window, only to find the space empty. One by one, I ventured through the cabins and found them all unoccupied. The only cabin that showed signs of recent activity was the one occupied by Morgan.

It was like he ran out in the middle of dinner. A half-eaten pizza sat on the counter. Dried up and disgusting, not even the flies were interested. If the petrified pizza was any indication, it had been sitting there for weeks. Sliding the fossilized food into the open trash can, I gathered the garbage and walked in the direction of my home. I had several mysteries to solve. First, who mowed my yard? Second, where exactly was Morgan? Third, where were my ranch hands, and fourth, where in the hell were my assets?

Expecting to be able to walk right in the door, I was caught off guard when the door stayed put and my forehead crashed into the wooden panel. Shouting expletives to myself, I unlocked the door and entered. Prominently placed on the table was a note.

Mickey,

I hope things went well at the bank. I mowed your yard. I also locked your door. You're going to have to get in the habit of doing that yourself. Your life seems to have taken a detour, don't let it completely derail you by being irresponsible. See you at six. I'll bring the wine.

Kerrick

I tottered between appreciation and annoyance. The man was totally frustrating. He showed up on the side of the road like a knight in shining armor—only this knight seemed more like a villain at times. He was bossy, pushy, and definitive in his resolve to bring me to heel. On the other hand, he was nurturing, attentive, and seemed to want me to step up and take control of my life. Why on earth did this man care about what happened to me?

Tossing the folder from the bank onto the table, I sat down and sketched out a plan.

Cattle Pros

Good source of income

Dad loved them

This was a cattle ranch

Cattle Cons

Time-consuming

Smelly

Dirty

Initial expense to purchase was cost-prohibitive

Transporting was a pain in the ass

I hated fucking cows

I sat and stared at the paper for minutes. The last sentence resonated all the way to my bones. I hated cows, always had and always would. The amount of cow shit that had been dragged through this house made me shudder. No wonder my mother took off and never returned. From the time I was seven, it was my dad, the crew and me.

Out of the corner of my eye, I glanced at Kerrick's business card and decided to send him a text.

Thanks for acting as my lawn boy.

Mickey

I see you got a phone. Good, that's a step in the right direction. As for the lawn, you're welcome. I found the mower in the barn. How's the plan coming along?

Kerrick

Do you ever take a break from nosing into other people's business?

If I was honest with myself, I had to admit that I was attracted to strong, dominant men. Kerrick projected the strength and confidence I found sexy. Did he possess control though? It was fine to be confident and strong, but to unleash your wrath on a woman was cowardly. Who abused those who were weaker than them? Morgan.

It's one of the hazards of being a detective. Get over it. I'm trying to help.

K

I told you earlier what kind of help I needed and you refused. Looks like I may be visiting Tommy's or Rick's Roost tonight.

M

It took ten minutes before he responded to my last message.

My refusal was based on my preconceived notion you were the dating type, which is something that doesn't interest me. Having a little sister, I view all girls as the dating type until proven wrong. I've been proven wrong. Can't stop thinking about you since you introduced me to some of your finer parts this morning.

Kerrick

So...he'd decided to get to know me better. This new information changed everything. With my phone in my hand, I raced to the bathroom to start the shower. There was no way I was having stubble on my first day back in the saddle. The beep of an incoming text message interrupted my preparation.

What are you doing? Did I scare you away?

No, I'm running a cold shower.

Use those razors. I don't want to get razor rash on my tongue. See you tonight.

I placed the phone on the old Formica countertop just above the burn scar where my hot curling iron had nearly eaten a hole through the top. That was another whipping that stayed fresh in my mind. Don't ever almost burn down the house.

Stepping past the lavender curtain into the shower, I leaned against the back wall and let the hot water stroke my body. With closed eyes, I imagined every drop of water cascading down my chest to be the flick of Kerrick's tongue. A tongue he'd offered up tonight as what? An appetizer—the main course? My fingers rolled over my breasts, and I wondered if his hands would be soft and sensual, or strong and demanding. Would he give as much as he took, or would he be like the others and take until I was empty? I pondered if his parts would match his big personality, or if he'd be like Morgan—Big M, little organ. My sex life had been a whole lot of nothing for over two years. Before that, it was barely worth a mention.

Starting at my toes, I worked the razor up each leg until my skin was silky smooth and stubble-free. Placing a liberal amount of body wash in my hand, I ran the suds between my legs. If there was even the slightest chance he was going to inspect my ladyscaping, I fully intended to make sure I was freshly mowed. The feel of my fingers as I spread myself apart stilled my breath. The spray of the showerhead pulsing against me had me clenching my teeth. I wasn't sure if I was reaching for release or pulling away. Coiled tension vibrated through my body, the feeling an echo of a past memory—a better time when all a girl had to worry about was getting caught in the barn.

Thoughts of the ranch flooded through me, effectively washing the arousal down the drain. Kerrick might be a good distraction, but that's all I could allow him to be. He was right, I needed to figure out what I was going to do with my future and the future of the ranch. It was all on me. The last time I depended on a man, it landed me in prison.

After a quick shampoo and good rinse, I dragged myself from the enveloping warmth of the shower and returned to my cold world.

Barefoot and dressed in shorts and a cotton shirt, I planted myself back at the table in front of my poorly laid out state of affairs.

"So, no cows. What does that leave?" I mumbled to myself. Twirling a long strand of hair around my finger, I inventoried my current assets.

Two thousand eight hundred seventy-four acres of land
One main house
Eight auxiliary homes with stables
One barn
One state-of-the-art stable for twenty-two horses and a fucking awesome arena
Saddles and tack for six horses
One beat-up ATV
One old truck
One working riding lawn mower
Family cemetery with ancestors turning in their graves.

Well, that about summed up the assets with the exception of the money I had in the safe, and the few thousand dollars I'd put in the bank. With only land and buildings, I needed to figure out how to make them work for me.

If I decided to go the cattle route again, I was going to have to take a loan out on the property. While not impossible, it would be tough, given my new, less-than-stellar credit rating. Who knew defaulting on every payment would lower a credit score by over two hundred points? That, combined with an arrest record, and I was persona non grata at the bank. On paper, I was a risk no matter what angle you came at me from.

With a notepad and a pen in my hand, I wrote about horses.

Horse Pros

Good source of income.

I loved them.

They were good company.

The ranch was well equipped for horses.

Minimal help required.

Horse Cons

Time Consuming.

Costly to house.

Needed help.

The ranch had no horses.

Looking at the list, I realized the pros and cons nearly canceled each other out. If the pros didn't get an extra vote because of my passion for the animal, then the list would be even. In all honesty, it would probably tip to the cons side once I factored in horses and heartbreak.

Laying my head on the solid wooden surface, I pounded my forehead gently into the table. The rhythm I adopted camouflaged the confusion in my brain.

"That bad, huh?" Jumping from my seat, I overturned the chair and faced the handsome man who entered my home with fists at the ready. "The door's unlocked, Mickey. I'm not happy." With a menacing scowl, he loomed over me. His very presence changed the atmosphere in the room. It crackled with energy.

"Shit, don't you knock?" Picking up the overturned chair, I placed it back at the table. If Morgan had stood over me that way, I'd have run to my room and locked the door. Why did I feel safer with Kerrick?

"I did, and no one answered, so I tried the doorknob and guess what? Unlocked." He tilted his head and rolled his eyes. "You can't continue to live without care. I swear I want to take you over my knee and spank you like an errant child." He placed two bags on the kitchen table and unpacked them while he appeared to wait for my response.

"You don't scare me, Kerrick." That statement actually surprised me. He had all the signs of a man capable of hurting me, and yet I didn't fear him at all. "I spent the last year in prison, where it was a daily challenge to survive. Prior to that, I had men who took great pleasure in making me pay for whatever perceived violation they thought I'd committed. One thing I've decided over the last year is I refuse to be broken." Was I warning him or reminding myself?

"What the fuck? I don't want to break you or beat you. I just want you to be safe." On the table, he placed two bottles of wine and a gallon of cream-colored paint.

"Sorry, I'm a bit stressed out. You should have come over an hour ago." In front of me sat the paint and wine, and I wondered what he had in mind. "I was in a totally different frame of mind. My brain was focused on meaningless sex, not survival." I disregarded his offerings as the conversation drifted to sex.

"Some would say sex is required for survival. It's an integral part of the human condition."

"Well, this girl hasn't been conditioned in a while." I put my hand over my mouth. Once again, I had talked without a filter.

"What, no lady loving in prison?" His eyes immobilized me with their savage intensity. "I've heard it's quite common." With a gentle push backward, Kerrick walked me back until he pinned me against the wall.

Dragging my eyes from him was like a workout. Every muscle strained to complete the task, but the pull of his weight was too strong. Stuck in his visual grip, I managed to answer, "It was an everyday occurrence. Two of my block-mates went after each other like fire to kindling. It wasn't for me, but after a year of listening to someone else getting off, you can imagine how frustrated I am." Natalie and my bunkmate went at it all the time. I couldn't bring myself to try it out. Natalie said it was a means to an end. She wasn't into girls, but she was into orgasms.

"Have you ever tried it?" His hips pinned mine to the wall. He nuzzled into my neck.

"No. Have you?" Pushing hard against his chest, he barely budged. The man was like a block wall.

"Eating pussy? Yes, I've tried it, in fact, I'm a huge fan. Sucking dick, no. I haven't tried it, and the thought makes my stomach turn. I can think of better things to do with a hard-on." Pressing himself against me, his hardness pressed into my hip. My breath hitched at the stone-like feel of his erection against me. My initial response was flight.

In a move that could only be learned from an expert, I gave a last-ditch effort at breaking free. I dropped my weight and twisted out of his grip. It was a move I'd learned from Robyn. Walking to the kitchen, I pulled the salmon from the refrigerator and sprinkled it with salt and lemon pepper. Cutting butter into small pieces, I put a small chunk on the top of each filet. I needed a few minutes to get used to the idea of what was about to happen. My body said go, but there was a thread of consciousness left in my brain that said no. It was teetering between *Hell, yes*, and *Uh oh*.

Coming up behind me, he whispered in my ear, "Why are you running?"

A tingling sensation poured over me like milk on cereal, no crevice was left unaffected. The desire for him had seeped into me completely. It had been over a year since a man had touched me, and several years since I had reacted with anything besides fear.

"I'm not running. I'm cooking dinner. I promised you a meal, and I intend to deliver." Oh, holy hell, his breath on my neck sent me straight to *Hell, yes*, and dinner seemed less important. "You're distracting me."

"Dinner can wait. I think you need to clear your head. I know a really good way to do that." His heated gaze made me flush with hot desire. "How about we work up an appetite, and then I'll help you cook?"

"What if I'm not interested?" Pulling my lower lip between my teeth, I waited.

He unbuttoned and unzipped my shorts. His hand made its way

down the front of my stomach, sending shivers down my spine and pulling a gasp from my mouth. His fingers slid inside my underwear and along my wet channel. I closed my eyes at his welcome intrusion. The feeling of his skin on mine pulled a low groan from deep inside. His manipulation of my flesh was quick and deliberate, and then he was gone. I peeled my heavy lids open to see his smiling face.

"I can feel how uninterested you are. If you were any less interested, you would have to mop the moisture running down your leg from the floor."

"Do you have to be so crude?" Pulling away, I buttoned up my shorts.

"I'm not crude, I'm honest. You want to be fucked. I want to fuck you. We both agree to the arrangement. It's just sex—filling an essential need. There is no shame in arousal. Shit, I've been aroused since this morning. The chafing of my underwear could make me come at this point. Besides, you brought it up."

He had me there. When it came to Kerrick, my mind had been gutter bound since I met him. "I can't help it. It's been years since I've been properly satisfied." My jaw dropped at my lack of verbal control.

"Why wait? Let's clear your head, and then we can sit and talk about your plan."

I growled at the mention of the plan. I had no plan, just a few pieces of paper outlining my dire circumstances.

With his arms encircling me from behind, he once again popped the button and unzipped my shorts. This time there would be no quick dip of his fingers and a dash away. His hand slid down my front for a slow and thorough exploration. With his finger placed strategically over my sensitive nub, he pushed me forward into the kitchen one step at a time. With every step, the shift of his hand was like slow torture, each move forcing his finger to drag against the inflamed tissue.

"Just a few more steps," he said, leading me across the linoleum floor. It wasn't like I had any choice. He had me pinned to him. "Pick up the food, and let's walk to the refrigerator." His voice skimmed over my skin like a silk glove. I did exactly as he asked. Everything felt too good not to yield to him. With the plate of salmon in my hands, I made it to the refrigerator weak-kneed and wobbly. "Good. Put it away."

The minute the door opened, he pressed his fingers deep inside of me. The plate toppled out of my hand and onto the top shelf of the refrigerator. It was as if that was somehow the plan all along. Collapsing against him, I leaned back and let him support my weight.

Warm lips came to rest at the crook of my neck. A soft tongue lingered endlessly over the pumping artery. What he wanted to do to me would take a very long time, he'd warned. I hoped he was a man of his word.

Turning me around, he pushed me against the counter and took my mouth in a rough and passionate kiss. All the while, his fingers slid rhythmically in and out of my moist passage. His free hand tugged and pushed at my shorts and underwear until they fell loosely to the ground at my feet.

He pulled my opening and dragged his fingers teasingly across my heated center. I felt the immediate loss of his connection. Without him there, the intense heat dissipated.

"Tell me, Mickey, if I make you come right now, will you be done, or is there hope for more tonight?"

"What? What do you mean?" Breathless, I steadied myself against the counter, trying to formulate a thought—any thought.

"Can you do multiples, or are you one of those girls who gets off and goes to sleep?"

Shaking my head, I tried to clear the confusion. He had created a sensual fog. It was a good place to be if you didn't have to talk. "I have no idea. All I know is, it's been a very long time since I've come, and usually it was just me. I'm a selfish lover and have never tried for multiples." *Oh my God, I just admitted to masturbating. Why do I tell him everything?* My face heated with embarrassment.

"Don't be ashamed. Let's see how far we can go. It would seem like you need sex worse than I do." And with that statement, he lifted me onto the counter and buried his face deep between my legs. The shock of his heated tongue exploring my most intimate parts sent fire ripping through my body. With gentle pulls and nips at my swollen flesh, he kept me teetering on the edge until tears pooled in my eyes. Grabbing the edge of the counter, I braced myself for the fall.

Shifting my hips to his satisfaction, he brought me to the edge of the counter and thrust his tongue deep inside of me. It was hot and slick and persistent. He took long, lingering licks over my sensitive flesh. I spread my legs wider to give him better access. Round and round his tongue circled the bundle of raw nerves, then he dipped inside to probe me thoroughly. My body buzzed with desire. The few brain cells still working marveled at how easily he aroused me. I'd never felt like this in my entire life. He sucked, nipped, pulled, and stroked—until the rush of sensation catapulted me over the edge. I grabbed the counter and white-knuckled the ride all the way down. I leaned limply against the cabinet until he pulled my body from the counter and carried me to bed.

With heavy eyes, he slid out of his clothes and pressed his naked body close to mine. His hands gently pulled at my shirt until it disappeared completely. Skilled fingers unhooked my bra with ease and laid me out completely naked in front of him. His eyes drank in every inch of me. Tight nipples rose to attention under his gaze. His tongue seared the puckered tips with a sweep of his mouth. Relentless in his attacks, he nibbled at the hardened pebbles in the same way he did the sensitive bud between my legs. The sensation built with each pass of his tongue. Every lick was a wake-up call to my senses. Holy hell, the man was good. I closed my eyes in bliss.

"Don't fall asleep on me." A growl delivered the warning.

"Or what?" Rolling on my side, I threw a leg over his hip. The prickly hairs on his thighs added to the sensation that was building inside of me. *Could I come again?* At the edge of that thought, I felt the unmistakable sting of his hand on my bare ass. The feeling, although shocking, was not unpleasant in my aroused condition. A small squeak escaped my lips to be replaced by a *hmmm*. He rubbed the tingle away with his roughened palm. I wasn't sure how I felt about his hand striking my bottom. It was hard to differentiate playfulness from the other.

"I owed you that for leaving the door unlocked, and now that that's out of the way, let's continue. I want you to touch me." He pulled my palm down to his groin, where I wrapped my fingers around his girth. *Definitely not a Morgan.* This man had it all: length and width and a hard body to boot.

"Will you suck me? I want your lips on me, just like I had mine on you."

I stiffened at his request. "No. I don't know where your thing has been. You knew mine had been in prison, but yours could have been in every vagina in Jefferson County." The thought made me squeamish.

His big eyes sparkled as he looked into mine, my hand continuing to rub his hard shaft. Mindlessly, I caressed him while he spoke. My fingers explored every vein, indent, and ridge. *Impressive.*

Breathlessly, he exhaled his answer. "I haven't been with anyone since my ex-wife. It's been a year. I don't want the complications of a relationship." My hand stopped its exploration at the word 'wife'. There was a stall while I processed his statement. Once my brain stored the 'ex' part of the sentence, my hand roamed freely again.

"A year is a long time." I knew what a year felt like. I lowered myself so I could tease the tip of his erection with my moistened lips. I knew that if he'd waited a year, then his need must be great. "You want my mouth here?" I purred. *Oh, what the hell.*

"Yes, I'm begging you. Take me into your mouth." In one swift movement, I enveloped as much of him as I could. The initial hitch in his breathing startled me, but the moan from his mouth elicited a response unlike any I'd felt before. His pleasure spurred me on to press more, suck harder. I was on a feeding frenzy, and this man was my meal. His carefully erected composure came undone with every pull of my mouth. His steely resolve and stony demeanor crumbled under the eager sucks and soft strokes of my tongue. Normally, the man was coiled tight with a different kind of tension. Today, he lay on my bed, straining with desire, and I controlled him with a flick of my tongue.

"Stop, or we'll be done. I'm not ready to be done." He tried to sound authoritative, but the power of his voice was lost in his need.

I reluctantly pulled my lips from the heated end of his length. I drew my body slowly up his to lie beside him, one hand pinned between our bodies, while the other was free to roam. Tracing his nipples, I listened to the sudden intake of air. Light as a feather, I ran my fingers up and down his body. His breathing settled to a more evenly paced rhythm.

Tight abs, well-developed chest muscles, and thighs of steel, this man was nearly a perfect specimen. His only bad quality was that he was too domineering, and the sad fact was, he was only looking for a toss in the sheets. Well, he gave an excellent oral presentation. Let's see if he could follow up with a hands-on demonstration.

"What do you like?" The question was picked from the air. One minute he was asking me to suck him deep into my mouth, and the next he was asking me what I liked. I'd never considered my likes to be part of the equation.

"I already got what I liked. Now, the rest is for you." Moving in closer, I took his nipple gently into my mouth.

"Ahh, that certainly does it for me. Does it do it for you, too?" His body shifted, popping his nipple from between my lips. With a gentle sucking motion, he drew the tip of my breast into his warm mouth. Savoring and suckling, he rolled the alert tissue across his teeth before he released it with a pop. Straining to return to the hot cavern of his mouth, my chest pressed forward, seeking him out. "I see that you like that, too. What else do you like?"

Frustrated at his desire to discuss rather than discover, I snapped, "What does it matter what I like? I generally don't get it anyway." Flopping to my back, I grazed my forehead with the back of my hand and released a breath full of disappointment.

"Look at me." He pulled my chin up to make sure I saw him while he spoke. "I don't know what you're used to, but you will get what you like, and you'll get it multiple times." His head dipped to my breast, and all thoughts and frustrations disappeared.

Writhing beside him, I shifted my body, trying to crawl under him. My entire body was awake—wide awake.

"I want you inside of me." The demand sounded foreign coming from my lips. I was a kitten, not a tiger, but something about this man demanded I become more. "Did you bring condoms?"

Shifting off the bed, he pulled a row of condoms from the front pocket of his pants. Stripping one free, he tossed the packet to me. I eyed the package and made quick work of opening it and applying it to his straining erection.

"There's no rush. We have all weekend if you like." Like a predator, he stalked to the end of the bed and glided up my body. Raining kisses and gentle flicks of his tongue up the inside of my legs, he journeyed to the juncture of my thighs, where he spread me wide and teased me until my center was hot and dripping. Grasping handfuls of comforter, I threw my head from side to side. I needed him to fill me completely.

"Now." I raised my hips off the bed with clear intent. "I need you, now," I cried out, desperation embedded in every syllable.

Poised above me, he balanced himself on strong arms, ready to enter me. His face was a contradiction between the hard line of his mouth and the softness in his eyes. I felt him push gently forward, nudging at my entrance. A feeling of fullness—completeness—covered me like a warm blanket.

"Look at me," he demanded.

My eyes shot open, and I was immediately caught in the vortex of his gaze. Intent to break the connection, I turned to the side and focused on the silver knobs of my dresser.

"Look at me, Mickey," he commanded more forcefully. "I want to see your passion. I want to know that I please you." He followed my eyes with his own. The intensity of his gaze was soul-ripping. *Could he see my fear? Could he sense my loneliness? Did he know what he was doing to my heart?* The thoughts kept racing through my head as he filled my void. Fully buried in me, I reached down to feel how tightly I surrounded his mass. At that moment, there was no beginning or end. We were one.

His deliberate pace and pressure made my body sing with pleasure. The not-so-familiar tingle slowly crawled up my spine. It clawed its way into my brain before it retreated back to my coiled, hot center. A shift of his hips and an increase in pressure were all it took for me to hurtle over the edge.

Afraid to close my eyes, I stared into his fixed gaze. Foreign sounds escaped my mouth in the form of whimpers and groans. He maintained his control until my last tremor passed. His eyes grew heavy, and his body shuddered. At that moment, I saw a glimpse inside this selfless man. My pleasure was all he required. *My pleasure was all he required.*

Chapter 6

MICKEY

Glistening with perspiration, Kerrick rolled to his side and murmured, "What do you like?" His hand trailed down my side, leaving goosebumps in its wake.

"I like you. I like what you did to me. I've never come simply from intercourse." *Did that really happen?*

"I don't do simple intercourse, that sounds so boring." He traced from my chin to my collarbone. "All the fun is in the build-up." My body quivered from his touch. "Your pleasure is my pleasure. With every stroke and every thrust, I'm determined to satisfy you."

"I am satisfied. Behind your demanding, egotistical, stubborn demeanor, I think you're a good guy, and I really like you." I turned on my side in time to see a frown flash across his face. In a hurry to change the tone of the moment, I blurted, "It's time to eat. I'm going to grab a shower. You can join me if you want, but it's a small shower, so you might want to wait." Hopping off the bed, I raced to the bathroom. With my back against the closed door, I breathed deeply. *How awkward was that? Best sex ever, but such a strange close to a wonderful experience.*

The smell of salmon drew me into the kitchen. I found him standing in front of my oven, cooking dinner. He masterfully flipped the filets over and placed them under the broiler. He was a beautiful sight, with nothing on but faded jeans that hung from his hips and cupped his butt perfectly.

"Have I been fired? I thought I was supposed to make dinner for you." Gliding past him to the cupboard, I reached for two plates and set them by the stove. I leaned against the counter to take in the sight once more.

"You look great in my kitchen." Giving him a sly wink, I took the silverware out of the drawer and placed it next to the plates. I was determined to make light of the awkwardness of our post-coital misunderstanding. He was gorgeous, but he was not permanent. I got that now.

"Listen, I don't want you to get—"

"Stop. I understand what this was. It was a quick one-night thing, and it's over. Let's not make it any weirder than it already is. I'm sorry if saying I liked you made you uncomfortable. It wasn't my intent." My chest tightened at the loss of what could have been perfect. He was perfect.

"I'm not relationship material. I was married, and it didn't work out." Pulling the broiled salmon from the oven, he set it on the stovetop and turned to me. "There are so many reasons why this wouldn't work." Turning back to the salmon, he plated up the fish and reached inside the refrigerator for the salad I'd prepared earlier in the day.

"Can you be hired on as a cook? You, mostly naked, cooking for me would be fabulous." I sang the last few words. Laughter broke the awkward silence.

"You can't afford me. Speaking of which, after dinner we need to go over your plan." He shuffled me toward the table and followed with two filled plates. He poured the wine and sat down.

"The key word in that sentence is 'your', meaning *my* plan. It's not Kerrick's plan, it's not the bank's plan, it's my plan, and honestly, I don't have one." I pushed the papers I was jotting notes on earlier in front of him.

"What did you do all day? Daydream about sex?" He placed a bite of salmon in his mouth and chewed.

"I hope you choke on a bone. I didn't spend the whole day dreaming about sex, just like an hour or so, but now that you've 'cleared my head', I might be able to come up with something solid. I did write down my assets and the pros and cons of owning livestock."

"Tell me what you think you can do with your assets. Eat while you're thinking, you're too skinny." Now we were back to the bossy Kerrick. I decided I liked the Kerrick who lay spent from passion better. That one kept his mouth shut.

"You didn't seem to mind my skinny ass twenty minutes ago." Shoving a piece of salmon in my mouth, I gave him a dark look.

"Obviously, I like what you have to offer, skinny ass and all. I don't do relationships, but I like sex." A glint of something crossed his face before his mask of indifference took over.

"Well, for being out of practice, I'd say that you deliver a good product." I hoped he changed his mind about the one-night thing. Tonight would go down in history as the best sexual experience of my life. Unfortunately, I let my heart be vulnerable for a moment, and something about him touched me. I was going to have to rein in my emotions when it came to him.

We finished our meal in silence. The quiet was a soothing balm for raw nerves. Focused on cleaning up after dinner, I didn't pay attention to what Kerrick was up to. When I turned around, he was shuffling small pieces of paper back and forth.

His eyes found mine across the room. For a moment, something connected but was quickly severed by his abrupt, "Get over here. This isn't going away."

With my head lowered, I walked slowly to the table and sat. Raising my knees, I pulled them to my chest and waited for him to tell me what to do.

"While you were cleaning the kitchen, I wrote each of your assets on a separate sheet of paper. Look at them and tell me which ones have earning potential, and which do not."

Lining up the papers in front of me, I analyzed them one at a time.

Family cemetery with ancestors turning in their graves.

"A bunch of graves are not going to pay the rent. We can discard this one." Fisting the scrap of paper, I crumpled it in my hand and tossed it aside.

"I concur." He took the stack in front of me and shuffled it. Pulling a paper from the center, he placed it on the table.

One main house.

"Unless I sublet the rooms or rent the property out, it has no income potential. I could sell the ranch, but that's not really an option, nor is it the objective." Crumbling the paper, I tossed it aside.

One beat-up ATV.

Crushing it, I threw it in the trash pile.

"What do you think you want to do for the rest of your life?" He handed me a pen and said, "Write down every idea you have for the remaining papers, no matter how crazy. You can do a second edit later." His question was thought provoking, and the only answer that came to mind was, I wanted to spend the rest of my life in his bed. *Hmm, sometimes life can be so unfair.*

"You might as well toss the truck and lawn mower in the pile. Selling them is the only option, and it won't pay the mortgage."

2874 acres of land.

I bit the end of the pen while I pondered the acreage. Once the ideas rolled through my head, I jotted them down without reservation.

Cattle
Sheep
Sublet for grazing
Fracking?
Water rights?
Crops-hay?
Eight auxiliary homes with stables
Rentals-long term
Summer rentals/vacation home
Summer camp
Conferences
Whorehouse

One barn
Storage
Dismantle and sell for scrap
Barn dance/community events

I tapped the pen on the table and stared at the paper in front of me. A bead of sweat trailed down my forehead and landed in a splash on the paper. Ink bled from the word 'stable'.

"Tell me why the stable causes you such pain?"

The tone in his question demanded an answer from me, but I refused to give in to a man who had no vested interest in my future.

"No, it's not your problem. Just drop it."

"Don't waste my time here. Let's get this done. Why do the stables throw you into a frenzy?" He pulled the pen from my hand and circled the word 'stables' several times.

Waste his time? I bristled at the notion that what we just experienced could have been considered anything but special.

"Sorry to be such a drain on your time. If I remember correctly, wasn't it you that pushed yourself into my life and my body?" The words *waste of time* replayed through my head. Wasn't that what I'd been all my life? Someone's waste of time?

"Shit, Mickey, you make it sound like my motivation was to get into your pants. I knew we should have waited. I knew you were under stress, and adding a relationship on top of it would be too much." He didn't sound angry. He sounded as if he was trying to convince himself that he tried to do the noble thing and somehow it was my fault things went too far.

"Don't confuse what we did with a relationship. It was a fuck, right? If you were my friend, I might have shared my deeper desires or hurts with you, but you're just a fuck, and as such, you don't get that privilege. We're done for the night. I'm tired, and I want to get some sleep. You know your way out. Lock the door behind you."

Pushing away from the table, I breezed past him and into my room, throwing myself on the bed. I heard a light tapping on my door.

"What?" Oh my God, did he have to make this any more difficult?

"I can't leave. You have the rest of my clothes in your room."

Grumbling to myself, I threw the door wide open, hitting the wall with force. A picture fell to the floor and shattered. Without a second glance, I climbed back into my bed and covered my head with the comforter.

The weight of his body dipped the mattress. The silence in the room was thick and heavy around us.

"I didn't mean to hurt you. I didn't mean to pry into your personal life. You're right, it's none of my business." The bed shifted, and his body slid next to mine. "I see a girl with no friends and limited resources. I thought I was helping. I want to be your friend, Mickey. I like you—everything about you." He pulled back the covers and pressed a kiss to my forehead. Strong arms pulled me to his chest and held me tightly. "You could never be just a fuck."

His words baffled me. His embrace comforted me. At that moment, I needed comfort more than clarity, so I snuggled into his side and fell asleep.

A LOUD CRASH from the living room sent me bolting from the bed. Quickly throwing on shorts and a shirt, I brazenly pushed forward. I'd no longer cower in the background while someone took from me. I refused to be a victim.

I raced into the living room, ready to do battle. Hands fisted as I screamed, "What the hell is going on in here?" Seeing Kerrick on the ladder was the last thing I expected.

"Sorry about the noise. I was trying to move the ladder, and I knocked over a chair. Go back to bed, it's early." *Now* he was worried about my sleep? Yesterday, he was happy to get me up at the crack of dawn.

"Have you forgotten I'm used to getting up early? What are you doing?"

"I'm covering your art." His eyes went to the spray-painted wall above his head. "This was undeserved and uncalled for, and when I find out who did it, I'll be doing some ass kicking. I protect my friends." With a toss of his head, he returned to the task at hand. A swipe of the brush over F U C left the words 'king bitch'. Looking at it, I saw that maybe there was some truth to it. Finding my inner bitch might help me be king. I'd heard it was good to be king.

"Can I get you some coffee?" Easing past the ladder, I entered the kitchen. "Where did you get the paint?" Pulling the grounds from the cupboard, I set up the pot and pressed brew.

"I found it in a storage closet at my apartment complex. It seemed like a neutral color. I hope it's okay I did this. It's my way of making up for being a dick last night." Climbing down the ladder, he took in his work and smiled like a kid who'd just gotten an A on his homework. Obviously proud of himself, he pounded the lid to the can closed and washed his brush.

"I'm sorry, too. You've been the only person who's been here for me, and I foolishly tried to run you off. Maybe you should have left the 'bitch' up there to remind me of what not to be." With two cups of freshly brewed coffee in my hands, I invited him to join me on the couch.

"I've known some real bitches in my time, and you're definitely not in their league."

"Oh, so I'm going to have to work on my skill set?"

"Please, don't. My bitch meter is maxed out for a lifetime." With a roll of his eyes, he sipped his black coffee. "Just the way I like it, fresh and strong."

"Anything you want to talk about? I'm an excellent listener." I gently tapped my nails on the mug, causing ripples to float across the surface. Wasn't it funny how the slightest disruption could create such a huge impact?

"No…actually, yes. As my friend, you should know a few things about me. I'm thirty. I got married when I was twenty-seven, divorced by twenty-nine. I know a few things about ranching, I grew up on one."

I processed the information and tilted my head. "You grew up on a ranch?"

With a howl of laughter, he responded, "I told you I was married, then divorced, and you zone in on the ranch."

"I've got priorities here. I have a ranch, you lived on a ranch, and we have something in common. Are you hungry?" I hoped he said yes. I was not quite ready to let him go.

"Yes, but before we move on to food, you need to know that we have a lot more in common than a ranch. We shared something amazing last night."

My heart shuddered in my chest. Thankfully, he recognized what happened between us. I was wondering if my time away had all but ruined my instincts.

"The salmon was good, but I wouldn't call it amazing," I said, knowing that he wasn't referring to the salmon at all.

"Now you're in trouble. You make me pour my heart out to you, and you bruise my ego in the process." In one swift move, he picked me up and placed me in his lap. "Now you need to kiss my bruised ego."

"Is that what we're calling it these days? If only a kiss were enough, you're a thorough man, and I don't see you stopping with a kiss. Tell me, if you're pouring your heart out to me, then tell me why you divorced her?" Although I was sitting on his lap, I felt like he was a million miles away. Turning his head to stare out the window, he spoke in a monotone. "She left me, said my job was my wife and there wasn't any room for her."

I took his face and pulled it toward me. "Was that true?" He was not the only one who could demand a look.

Thoughtfully, he looked into my eyes and said, "Yes, I'm married to my job, but no more than anyone else is married to theirs. If you decide on your life's work and give it less than your all, then what's the point?" His expression turned into sadness, and then regret. "I felt the same about my marriage, but despite my best efforts, I couldn't give her everything she wanted, and she eventually found someone else who could."

"I'm sorry. Relationships are hard." My experience with Morgan should have made me shy away from everyone, but I refused to abandon the possibility of falling in love. "I can understand why you're so opposed to commitment. I don't have such a great success record myself." My choices had left a scar on my heart that I fought to heal daily.

"It's not that I'm opposed, I'm not certain my lifestyle is conducive to a healthy, committed relationship. I also have huge trust issues. It's another thing we have in common." His gentle fingers pushed back the hair from my face. "You looked like a mad woman when you flew out of your room. Your hair flying behind you made you look like a woman possessed."

"It's a good thing we agreed to just be friends, because telling a girl she looks like a crazed madwoman won't get you anywhere but in trouble." Pulling at my hair, I tried to get the curls under control.

"You're beautiful, crazy hair or not." Winding a ringlet around his finger, he pulled it down and let it spring back. "Where did you get these curls?"

"A gift from my mom." I tried to move from his lap, but he held my hips in place.

"Don't move. I like you where you are." Fixing his eyes on me, he asked, "Where is your mom? She's not buried here, so I surmise she's still alive. It baffles me to think about where she is when you need her so much." His detective skills had no boundaries, and his questions continued to open old wounds.

"I don't need her. She left us when I was really little. Told my dad that he was married to the ranch, and she felt like a jealous mistress." What mother left her daughter? *A bad one,* my inner voice told me. "So you see, we have another thing in common. Someone we loved left us because they wanted to be the center of the universe, rather than a participant in the grand plan." Would my life have been different if I'd had the wisdom of a woman guiding me? I'd never know.

Soft lips touched mine in a tender kiss while strong hands pulled me into a reassuring hug.

"As much as I'd love to sit here on your lap and let you kiss me dizzy, we don't have that kind of relationship. Thanks for painting my wall. I'll cook you breakfast, and then you need to be on your way. You're way too distracting to me."

"I'm glad, for both things. Actually, all three: breakfast, dizzying kisses, and distraction. Are you sure you don't need my help?" His question sounded more like a pleading for me to ask for help, rather than dismiss him outright.

"Unless you have a few experienced ranch hands in your back pocket, I fear the only help you can give me will be manual labor. I'm happy to make a list if you're interested. I can't pay you, but I can feed you." It was one way to keep him around. I wondered if I worked him hard enough, would he collapse in bed beside me at night? It was a thought.

"What if I could provide you with ranch hands and help you with the manual labor? Would you barter for something more valuable than a meal?" He smiled a sexy, I've-got-something-up-my-sleeve smile. Who could resist that?

"Come into the kitchen and talk to me." I walked to the refrigerator and removed the eggs, cheese, and ham. "What did you have in mind?" I cracked the eggs into a bowl. It was such a normal thing to do, but something I'd taken for granted for so many years.

"I know you're thinking I'm asking for sex, and maybe I am. I'd love that. Sex with you is amazing, but I wouldn't presume to think you'd be interested after last night." Taking the eggs from my hands, he scrambled them with vigor. "I have a horse, and I'd much rather board him here than where I have him. I'd also want to ride him on your land. I'll pay you a boarding fee if you look after him." This was about his horse. He *did* say something about sex as well. *Did he say it was amazing?* That had merit.

"You have a horse? What kind of horse?" Tossing the diced ham and cheese into the scrambled eggs, I poured the mixture into the heated pan.

"A Quarter Horse. You can take the boy out of the ranch, but you can't take the ranch out of the boy."

"What kind of ranch?" I felt his hands on my hips and his chin on my shoulder. Leaning over my body, he watched me cook. I liked the feel of him next to me. Damn man. If he continued to do things like this, how was I supposed to resist him?

"Horse ranch, mostly Quarter Horses, but some Appaloosa and

Paint as well. I come from a family of breeders." His comment made me laugh.

"I saw your talents last night, and I imagine your breeding skills are highly sought after." With a push of my hips, I forced him to back away so I could plate up our breakfast.

"Are you teasing me? In answer, I'm highly sought after, but rarely caught." He took the plates off the counter and walked them to the table. "I'm very selective."

I followed with toast and coffee. "Oh yeah, I can see how selective you are. You pick up a strange girl outside of a prison and make her your choice. Someone has got to give you a lesson on where to find women. I know it's been a year, but you're going to have to be more responsible." It gave me great joy to throw his words back at him.

"Really? You're going to give me a lesson on being responsible? This coming from a girl who left a douchebag in charge of her ranch and didn't lock her door? Please," he responded with an exaggerated toss of his head.

"I didn't have a choice about who was left in charge of the ranch. I was arrested and sentenced right away. The door thing... I'll have to work on that. It's hard to break a twenty-four-year habit."

"Ah, so you're twenty-four. Finally, a morsel of information I can use. I was beginning to think I might have to run a background check on you."

"You wouldn't do that, would you?" A look of indignation crossed my face. "I mean, isn't that invasive and unfair, not to mention probably illegal?"

"Something you don't want me to know? We're becoming friends, and friends should be open and honest with each other." *Was there something specific he wanted to know?*

"No, I have nothing to hide. You can ask me anything you want." Once the words were out of my mouth, I regretted them immediately. What little I knew of Kerrick, I did know that he wouldn't stop with the questions about the horses and stable. It wasn't a big secret, just a painful truth.

"Tell me about Morgan. Are you, or were you in love with him?" The question jolted me. It wasn't what I expected. In fact, a discussion about Morgan could prove to be more painful than one about the stables.

"No, I'm not in love with him. Yes, there was a time I thought I loved him, but he showed me his true colors shortly after my dad passed away. He was not a nice man. If you want to exercise your investigative talents, then find out where he went. I've been told he's following the rodeo circuit, but I'm not certain he has the level of commitment that that takes. Besides, he owes me four hundred fifty head of cattle and a shitload of money."

"Four hundred fifty head of cattle is a small herd for the land you own. I imagined you would have had at least one thousand head. What happened?"

"That was the plan. We used to have a larger herd when my dad was alive. We were supposed to increase in cattle to eighteen hundred this year. My dad took an equity loan on the ranch in order to upgrade the houses for our cowboys. We were in expansion mode, more cattle, more horses. When he died, several of the hands left and expansion got put on hold."

Reaching for the pages I wrote on last night, I pushed the plate away and set the papers in front of me. "There were four remaining cowboys when I went away. Now, I have none. However, I do have eight really great cabins and a ranch without any animals." I scrunched my nose and shook the depressing information from my brain.

"I can get you two experienced hands right away. They can be here within a week. What do you want to ranch?"

Here it was, the big question of the moment. I knew that cattle were out of the question, but would that be disrespectful to my family who had raised cattle here their whole life?

"If you're truly trying to be my friend, I need your advice." I tore the corners of the page, making the sheet smaller as if it would do the same to the dilemma. "My family has raised cattle on this ranch for over a hundred years. Is it disrespectful to go in a different direction? I'm pretty much tossing aside everything they'd worked for."

He sat for minutes, seeming to contemplate his answer. "I can only tell you what it's like for me. My family has raised horses for over a century. My ancestors came from Ireland without a penny to their name. They purchased land in Wyoming and became horse traders through thievery." Twisting his neck from shoulder to shoulder, he continued. "My great grandfather stole some of the finest horses around the country and bred them on his own. The ranch wouldn't be there now if generation after generation didn't follow through and keep it going." He pulled the rapidly shrinking page from my hand and laid it back on the table. "Having said that, would the world be worse off to have one less horse ranch?"

"Why aren't you running your ranch?"

"Although we're Irish through and through, my family is much like English nobility. You have an heir and a spare. In our case there was an heir, three spares and a daughter thrown in for good measure." Reaching out, he took my hands in his. "What I'm saying is that for me, it wasn't a matter of continuing a family legacy. I wasn't going to inherit the ranch anyway. I went into law enforcement because I love figuring things out." He turned my palms over and rubbed against the soft pads of my fingers. "I owed it to myself more than I owed anything to my family. No matter what you decide, as long as you hold on to the land, you will still be a ranch owner. You just have to decide what these hands want to do." He let my hands slip to the table.

"That's the problem. I have an empty ranch."

"Whether it's bees or buffalo, it's still a ranch. Sometimes, changing things can make it better. You have to find out what works for you. Changing the direction of your life is not a tragedy; losing the passion for living it is. Even if you decide that ranching isn't for you and you want to sell the land, you have the right to live a happy life."

Wow, the man was smart and sexy. Who knew? I thought about his words momentarily, but the initial thought I blurted out anyway.

"I hate cows," I said without reserve.

"Then scratch cows off the list." He took a pen from the table and marked a solid line through 'cattle' on the paper that said 2874 acres of land.

"I love horses, I always have. I just have a lot of guilt surrounding them, but I'd consider horses again. Who are these ranch hands you were referring to?"

"Keagan and Killian can be here in a week."

The names were a dead giveaway. They could only be his brothers. "Are they cute, like you?"

"No, they're ugly as trolls. One has webbed hands, and the other has hideous facial warts. However, they do have horses and a set of skills that could be valuable to you. Killian is one the best horse breeders in Wyoming. He would be an asset to your ranch. Keagan is an excellent trainer."

"Why would they come here when they already have a job in Wyoming? How do I pay them?" It was the same problem each time. No help. No money. No hope.

"Both are looking for an opportunity to establish themselves outside of the family name. What about offering them a place to live and housing for their animals? You could give them a portion of the profits of the ranch."

"There is no profit."

"That's the beauty of it. You won't owe them anything until the ranch starts making money, and since they have an interest in the success of this new endeavor, they will be motivated to make it work. My brothers have been looking for a chance to break away from home. If you want to dangle a carrot, tell them you'll cook." He picked up the plates and walked into the kitchen.

I sat and stared at the one piece of paper I didn't address yesterday. Picking it up, I read the words. *One state-of-the-art stable for twenty-two horses and a fucking awesome arena.* Underneath, I wrote down ideas.

Horse Boarding

Riding lessons

Barrel racing and roping training

Horse rescue

Breeding?

"Now you're on to something. I pay $650 a month to board Keen, and it's not nearly as nice of a place as you have here. I'd much rather board Keen here if you'll take him. I know you wanted me to leave, but since I plan to board my animal here, I have an interest in making sure the stables are in good condition. Should we work on them together?"

"Call your brothers and see if they're interested. There is no use in moving forward if I don't have help. I need to go and talk to Daddy for a few minutes. I'll meet you in the stables in an hour. Don't start without me."

Just as I was beginning to assume my life was derailed permanently, Kerrick offered up his family. I thought about his decision and glowed with warmth and a bit of pride. Surely, he wouldn't bring them here if I didn't have something to offer them.

Chapter 7

MICKEY

I sat beside my father's grave, picking at the newly sprouted weeds. Too bad opportunities didn't grow as fast as grass. Sucking in a breath of courage, I began.

"Hey, Daddy. Do you remember when you told me that the one thing I could count on was change? Well, things are changing. I tried to keep up with the cattle, but I failed. I never did like those stupid cows."

I sat against the granite headstone and blanketed the patch of land with my long legs.

"I came to a decision today with the help of a friend. The ranch is changing. I hope you won't be disappointed in the direction I take it. Tomorrow, I'm going to visit Tom Morrow and see if he wants to lease the lower two-thirds of the range. It's good grazing land, and I'm sure his cattle will be happy there. It will provide a steady income that can help finance other pursuits. Hopefully, by next week I'll have a few hands around to help me out."

A ray of sunlight peeked through the burgeoning clouds, and I took it as a good sign.

"I'm going to open the stables again. It's my only hope of

holding on to the ranch. Please watch over me, and the people who live here. I love you, Daddy, and I hope to make you proud."

The wind whipped through my hair as if my father's fingers had brushed past it. Was it a whisper of support? Running my hand over the curls, I rose and glanced down at his grave. "I'm sorry I wasn't with you when you passed. I should have been there. I won't let you down again."

"Don't let pain and grief be a thief. They will steal your future." Warmth blanketed me as the memorized phrase circulated through my brain. It was always my father's way of telling me to move forward without regret.

I found Kerrick leaning against the stable door. Dressed in blue jeans, a button-down shirt, and boots, he was picture perfect. He must have had a change of clothes in his truck. Looking like he was ready to saddle a horse and ride, I giggled.

"What are you laughing at?" Pushing off the door, he strode toward me.

"I was thinking about the empty stables and how disappointing the morning will be for you. All dressed up, and nothing to ride."

"Well, that all depends on what you have in mind. I'm quite talented when it comes to mounting a filly, and I see a beautiful one standing in front of me." Of course, he was going to taunt me with sex. Talk about dangling a carrot.

"Do men ever think about anything other than sex?"

"Yes. We think about food and fast cars. How was your visit?" He walked forward, raising his hand to brush the hair from my face. I shrank at his gesture. Turning quickly, I evaded his touch. With him a safe distance behind me, I answered his question.

"He didn't have much to say, but I let him know things were changing. How was the phone call?" I beat a path into the stable and threw open the stalls.

"They'll be here next week. They're bringing several horses, I hope that's okay. They're excited. They've wanted to come to Colorado for a while." He grabbed a broom from the wall and swept the stalls. "Outside, I tried to touch your face and you cowered. Does that have anything to do with me or is it something else?"

I paused in my work, stunned that he'd noticed what I thought was an imperceptible reflex. How did I answer him?

"It's not you. I grew up with a bunch of men who played rough. I thought you were going to chuck me on the chin." Protected by the wall of wood that separated us, I pitched my lie.

"Hmm. You know I'm a detective, right? You can toss your load of manure as far as you want to throw it, but in the end it remains shit. I'm calling bullshit, Mickey." He walked to the stall I was hiding in and found me leaning against the wall. "I'll give you the afternoon to think about it, but I want an answer. I pretty much have it figured out. Are you sure you want me to find him? When I do, I may have to kick his ass."

"Let it go. We have a lot of other things to occupy our time and energy. There are twenty-two stalls that need to be swept out. After that, we have eight houses and more horse stalls to clean. No complaining, you volunteered."

"Yes, I did. Why don't you open the doors and windows to air the place out? It smells like sour hay."

THREE HOURS and two blisters later, I dragged him toward the exit. A few steps in, I tripped over a shovel. "You need to put things back." I picked it up and hung it in its place before I walked out the door and to the main house. I quickly grilled a few chicken breasts and sliced two peaches. It wasn't a lot, but it was a meal. I'd definitely have to hit the grocery store later. My eyes caught him sliding the soft, juicy flesh of the peach into his mouth.

"You're right. These are perfect. They taste as good as they smell—just like you. Last night I inhaled you—" he sniffed the air as if reminding himself, "—and you smelled sweet and sexy. I. Had. To. Suck. Your. Sweet. Juices." Hearing him say those words so slowly caused me to moisten in the place he'd just mentioned. But I was determined not to succumb to his seduction.

"You're so gross. No girl wants to hear about her juiciness." Not this girl. Not right now anyway. Crumbling my napkin, I wound up for a strike and hit my target head-on. Let the games begin.

"You didn't just hit me, did you? It's not possible. If you actually did, I'd have to retaliate."

Watching him twitch, I saw the look of anticipation light up his face. He was like a hungry cat ready to pounce on a cornered mouse. I decided my best plan of action was to escape and evade. Dashing to my right, I tripped over my feet trying to get to the kitchen. I was sprawled flat on the floor when he straddled me and pinned me in place. "Don't run from me, Mickey. I'll always catch you." With the flexibility of a gymnast and the strength of a weightlifter, he shifted my body so he could remove my pants and underwear with ease. Propped on my knees, his fingers floated down my stomach and dipped into me. Wet with desire, I rolled my hips with shameless abandon.

I knew he would catch me, the chase was half the fun. "Are you ready for that ride, Cowboy?" The huskiness in my voice sounded like I'd had a two-pack-a-day habit for years.

Pulling his glistening fingers from between my legs, he held them in front of my eyes. "Are you going to tell me you're not wet? This is fucking sexy, Mickey. You're wet for me. I made you this way, so when I tell you that you're juicy, it's a compliment. I may as well have just told you that you control my dick."

I turned to him, opened my mouth, closed it, and then opened it again. When I began to speak, he silenced me with a kiss. Between gulps of air, I asked, "Do you love this shirt?" My fingers traced the buttons down his chest.

"I like it, but I'm not in love with it. Why?"

Too impatient to unbutton his shirt, I gripped both sides and pulled with the strength of a hundred men. Buttons flew in every direction and settled on the floor like spinning tops that had lost their momentum, wobbling until they fell flat.

"I've always wanted to do that." My hands slithered beneath the material to his chest. He pulled the remainder of his shirt from his body. My fingers explored the firmness of his muscles.

Hell be damned with a one-night stand, I was stealing another day.

"How are you so confident in some places in your life, and not in others?" His question interfered with my exploration.

"Are you confident in everything you do? Are you always self-assured, or do you hide behind a mask of conviction?" I fingered the small scar that ran low across his ribcage. I questioned him with my eyes.

"Sword fight with Keagan when I was eight. I lost. I was confident that I'd win. I was wrong."

"Does it pain you to be wrong? We're all wrong sometimes."

"We're not talking about me, we're talking about you. Why do you cower? Are you afraid of men?"

"Do you really want to talk about my past relationships? I thought you wanted to ride." Reaching down, I cupped the bulge in his pants and squeezed it for emphasis. Flipping me around, he settled me on my hands and knees in front of him. His buckle hit the floor, followed by the soft swish of fabric. The sound of tearing foil filled the air. I closed my eyes and waited expectantly, the excitement making me tremble.

His coarse hairs grazed the back of my legs. Calloused hands roamed across my backside just before he gripped my hips. He lined up with my aching entrance and plunged deep inside of me. A sigh of satisfaction broke free. He pounded relentlessly into my sex. So close, and yet I couldn't break free and fly. Every bad moment in my life was temporarily released thrust by thrust. I strived to feel full and yet empty at the same time.

"Come for me, Mickey. I don't know how long I can keep this pace."

"I can't," I cried, frustrated my body wouldn't give me what I needed.

"You can, and you will." The forcefulness of his voice called my body to action. Trembling beneath him, he gave my sex a rough pinch, sending me soaring over the edge. He stilled, buried deep inside me, allowing my body to pulse around his hardness. Firm hands grasped my hips, and the pounding began anew. Spent, I laid my upper body flat on the floor. I gladly submitted to this man who dominated my senses. One…two…three powerful strokes later, he shuddered his release, collapsed against me, and forced us both to the cold floor.

In the silence, I thought about him. For the first time, a man had given me more pleasure than pain. *Don't go there, Mickey. Stay detached. Jobs. Lots to do.* I coaxed myself away from the confusing bliss I was feeling.

"We should get dressed. There's still a lot of daylight left, and I can't waste a minute. I've got help on the way."

"Why are you always in a hurry to get away from me?"

It wasn't that I wanted to distance myself, it was that I couldn't separate my heart from my body. Telling him my truth would make him run, and that would hurt too much.

"I'm not. I'm in a hurry to get my life on track. You're a distraction. A very good one, but lying on the kitchen floor with you isn't going to get the houses ready for your brothers. Tell me about them." I hoped my question would redirect his thoughts.

"I'll make you a deal. I'll tell you about my family, but you have to reciprocate in kind. I want to know about the people who raised you."

A frown pulled at the corners of my mouth. "Fine," I said curtly.

He talked as we dressed. He tucked his torn shirt into his pants. It fell open where the buttons were gone. "My parents are Kane and Kathryn McKinley. Keanan is the oldest, then me, Keagan, Killian, and then Keara. Don't ask, I have no idea why the K names, only that my parents' first names started it all. Shit, I even named my horse Keen, but it was because he's smart. The little bastard is like Houdini, I have to padlock him in his stall because he escapes. I think he wants to run like a wild Mustang. I can't blame him. I wouldn't want to be tied down either."

Ouch. Got it.

"I wish I had siblings. It would have been easier to get through things if I weren't so alone. I've been the only girl on this ranch for almost two decades. Sure, there was the occasional barfly that buzzed around the cabins, but nobody ever stayed. The men took what they needed and sent them packing." I hopped across the floor, pulling my boots on. "I was off limits until Morgan. I think my dad figured out I was dating whether he liked it or not, so he intervened and set me up with him. He was new to the ranch and a hard worker. He was a rodeo champion, and my dad saw the potential in him."

"What's his specialty?"

"Bending strong headed animals to his will." Chewing my lip, I pulled my pants over my boots and walked to the door. "He roped animals. He was very good."

"Why did you let him hit you?" He followed closely on my heels as I marched toward the cabins.

"I didn't *let* him hit me. The first time it happened, I was shocked into silence. After that, I was too ashamed to admit it was happening. I wasn't a weak girl, I was just a stupid one." We crossed the threshold of the first cabin. "You don't know Morgan. He's big like you, but mean. He was quite charming in the beginning, and I think my dad saw himself in Morgan, maybe the son he never had."

"If he wanted a son so badly, why didn't he and your mother have more children?"

"Complications at birth. I left my mom unable to bear other children." I threw open the window to let fresh in. "Don't get me wrong, he didn't love me less. He was a good father."

"Was he abusive?" I reflected on his question for a moment. So many things these days are considered abuse, but as a child, you only know what's normal to you.

"I wouldn't call him abusive. He was firm and rigid. He never hit me with his hands, but I did feel the leather of his belt across my ass more than a few times." I cringed at the memory.

"I'm sorry, Mickey. You've had a tough life." Stopping me as I filled a bucket with water and pine cleaner, he pulled me in for a hug. I stood rigidly against him, unwilling to accept his warmth and empathy. Empathy had never been an emotion my father had, so I wasn't used to it now. Pushing away, I picked up the bucket and wiped down the counters.

"I'm good. My biggest problem is that I've depended on too many men to make things work for me. I didn't have many options then, but I have choices now. I need to depend on myself from now on. If I acted more like a man, I might not be in the pickle I'm in now."

"You don't have to act like a man to be strong. All you need is a plan and the backbone to stick with it. Look what you've done in a few days. You took a failing ranch and gave it potential. You're facing your fears head-on. I'm proud of you."

My heart swelled with emotion.

"Thanks for that. You've helped me see things in a different light." How was it that this man saw my potential as no man before him could? "I may still lose the ranch, but it won't be because I didn't try to save it."

We worked side by side in relative quiet. With two cabins scrubbed from top to bottom, I felt good knowing that Keagan and Killian would have a clean place to stay.

"They're going to love these. You guys did a great job remodeling." He walked slowly through the freshly cleaned space. "Are they all two bedrooms?"

"Yes—" The song "Bad Boys" filled the air, and Kerrick scrambled to get his phone out of his pocket.

"Detective McKinley."

He paced the room. Single words like *yes* and a sarcastic *perfect* floated around the cabin. Feeling uncomfortable about eavesdropping, I pointed toward the door and left him to his work while I returned home.

Fifteen minutes later, he knocked at the front door to the main house. The serious look on his face told me he was on his way somewhere else. Something bad had just gone down.

"I've got to run, there was a bank robbery." This was what my life would be like if he gave it a chance. "I'm sorry to leave you with the other cabins, but I have to go. I have no idea when I'll be around again." I thought about the amount of time he had spent with me in relation to the time he had to work. It seemed like a decent trade-off. What the hell was his ex thinking? "I'll call when I can." He leaned in to plant a gentle kiss on my lips before he walked to his truck and took off toward town.

THIS MORNING, I felt confident. The night before, I'd spent hours researching grazing fees on the Internet. With solid information, I was empowered to strike a fair deal with Tom.

Meeting with Tom Morrow was like picking off a scab slowly. Each question peeled back a layer of sorrow. Each reflection left a stinging ache. Each memory left my heart raw and bleeding. The conversation with him resembled a ping-pong game with both players volleying for control. It seemed more like a trip down memory lane than a meeting to negotiate a land contract.

"You've always been a wild child, Mickey. When are you going to settle down and take your life seriously?" I'd admit to being spirited at times, but a stern look or a warning always tamed me.

"Mr. Morrow, I've never been a wild child. I was raised by men and therefore don't have that softer edge you learn from time spent with women. I work hard and play hard. Yes, I can swear like a sailor, but never think I don't take my responsibilities seriously." I wondered what he was getting at.

"Your choice to sell off the cattle was stupid. What would your dad have said?" *Ah, the cattle.*

We sat on his front porch and talked. "I didn't choose to sell the cattle. They were gone when I got home." The conversation was turning out to be as unpleasant as the scent the wind carried from his herd. "As for my dad, I have no idea what he'd think, but he didn't raise a quitter. You're an integral part of my new plan. I need your business to finance my future. Shall we talk numbers?"

The negotiations began at fifteen dollars per head and ended up at nine per animal when the deal was finalized. Tom agreed to maintain the fences and to shift his cattle between pastures on a regular schedule. The only thing I needed to do was collect the check.

I secured access rites to the trails at the far end of the property.

Wanting nothing to do with the cows, I felt like I had negotiated well. With 1248 head of cattle in his herd, Tom would be keeping my ranch afloat until a better plan could be devised.

The next stop on my list was Dr. Mallory. He had taken over the veterinary practice while I was in prison. He kindly made time for me on his day off. It was rare for someone to go out of their way for a stranger, and on a Sunday no less.

I saw him standing in front of the building as I pulled up. Dressed in khakis and a collared shirt, he could have just walked out of church.

"Dr. Mallory?" With a tilt of my head, I processed his face and attributes. It was like thumbing through a mental Rolodex, looking for the one card buried in the middle. I saw familiar green eyes, but it was hard to reconcile him with the fat boy from my childhood who called me names.

"Hi, Mickey, how are you? It's been such a long time since I've seen you."

"Wow, Roland, you've slimmed down. I guess I can't call you Roly Poly anymore. How are you?" I scanned him from head to toe and couldn't believe the chubby boy that spent one day a month at the ranch teasing me unmercifully was the same man in front of me now. Tall and lanky, he'd come a long way from the annoying little porkster of my youth.

"I'm good. How are you, Pigeon?"

"You will not call me Pigeon." Shaking my head, I narrowed my eyes at him and set out to correct the error of his ways. "Your dad was cruel to make fun of my skinny legs. I suffered years of taunting because of something I couldn't control. I'd have happily traded my legs for kneekles and cankles."

He took me in and focused on my legs. "Looks like we both outgrew our childhood shortcomings."

"Well, I still have long, gangly legs, but the boys don't seem to be bothered by them anymore."

"I bet." His appreciative glance lingered on me a bit longer than necessary, sending a flush of embarrassment across my face. "I'm here because I'm changing things at the ranch, and I wanted to secure your services."

"Okay, but you said on the phone that Morgan had sold all the cattle, and the ranch was currently an animal-free zone. Why would you be in need of a vet?"

"Starting next week, I'll be taking in horses for boarding." I leaned against my truck and crossed my ankles. "I have a breeder and a trainer coming from Wyoming. With twenty-two stalls that need occupants, I'd like to be able to advertise you as the on-call equine specialist. I want to make sure my clients feel confident that every need will be met."

Roland sidled up next to me. We faced his veterinary clinic. It appeared the same as when it belonged to his father. "My dad always talked about you. He said that you were quite the horse-woman. Aren't you like a champion barrel racer or something like that?"

"Something like that. I haven't ridden for a couple of years. I wouldn't even consider bringing horses into the mix again, except that I may lose the ranch, and horses are all I know. I have to use the resources I have. So what do you say? Will you sign on to be my vet?"

"I'd be happy to look after the animals on the ranch in exchange for a favor. There are still lots of homeless horses due to the fires that swept through Waldo Canyon and the Black Forest. Many owners were not able to rebuild and have relinquished their animals. Would you be willing to adopt a few horses? I could help you find a few good tempered ones. Who knows? They could turn out to be great training horses." His expression was hopeful. I knew what that looked like and felt like. "You'll need to get back in the saddle again if you're going to give riding lessons."

"Oh no, I don't plan to do that. I'm just going to house the horses and care for them. My riding days are over." I wondered if it would be possible to have horses on site and not want to ride them. *Could I?* It would mean working through my self-doubt and grief.

"Having your own mount will give you credibility in the marketplace. Besides, you are a bit of a celebrity in these parts. Between the awards you've earned and the incarceration, lots of people know you. Curiosity alone will bring them to the ranch. So, what about the horses? Should I put my feelers out?"

Kicking myself from the inside out, I realized he was right. "Yes, please." Everything was leading back to horses.

We finalized our agreement with a handshake and a promise to call him as soon as I had animals on board. I headed off to take care of my final chore for the day.

Chapter 8

MICKEY

It was my second time at the grocery store, and it felt almost as exciting as the first. The only difference was, Kerrick was missing from the mix. I hadn't heard from him since yesterday, when he left my house wearing a tattered shirt and a menacing scowl. I'd put the tattered shirt there. However, the scowl came from a phone call that interrupted our plans.

I picked up some fresh fruit and salad fixings before I made my way to the meat department. The prospect of dining alone saddened me. I set a steak and a chicken breast side by side and snapped a picture with my phone.

Would you care to join me for dinner? I'm at the grocery store and was thinking about you.

M

I pressed send and waited for his response. Almost immediately, I heard the chime of an incoming text.

I wish I could, but I'm swamped at work. I was hoping to get some time to look into the whereabouts of Morgan. What's his last name again?

K

Disappointment weighed me down. I tossed the single servings of meat into my cart and responded.

Set Free

Canter. Morgan Canter. Don't work too hard. Maybe I'll see you soon.
M

I tossed my phone into my bag and resumed shopping. Why did I crave his company so much? Was it the sex or the man? Analyzing my feelings, I stood in line to check out.

"You're back." My eyes rose to the cashier's face. It was just my luck I got the same cashier as the other day.

"A girl's gotta eat." Trying to expedite the process, I bagged my groceries.

"Maybe you should wait just in case you need to put something back." Her snide remark rubbed me in the worst way. "Your man isn't here to save the day." Looking around to see who was within hearing distance, I found us alone at the register.

"What the hell is your problem?" My voice took on the sound of a woman possessed. "I don't even know you, except that maybe we went to the same high school. What's your issue with me?"

"You don't recognize me, do you?" She tossed her hair over her shoulder. The way it flew through the air brought instant recognition. She was the girl from the car, the one who was perched on the hood like an ornament. She was the one whose eyewitness account sent me to prison for a year.

"Yes. Yes. I know who you are now. I hope that a lousy fuck with Morgan was worth tossing my life aside for a year. You knew what happened that night, and yet you lied to save his ass. You weren't the first woman he brought to the house to taunt me, but you were the last."

"You did slash his tires and hit him with the tire iron. That's all I testified about." She shrugged her shoulders with indifference.

"You do realize that fucking you on the car was the smallest thing that happened that night, right? He beat me senseless." She cringed at my last statement. "It's over and done. You did what you felt you had to do. End. Of. Story." I bagged my own groceries. "By the way, do you have any idea where Morgan is? He basically embezzled enough money to send him away for years. It seems fitting, doesn't it?"

"I haven't seen that asshole since the day he split my lip." Her confession didn't surprise me, nor did it gain her sympathy points.

"Well, looks like he took something from both of us. He probably took your trust and self-respect. As for me, he tried to take everything." She finished ringing up the groceries. "If you see him, tell him I want my money back." I paid the bill with cash and headed home.

As soon as I entered the house, I turned around and locked the door. Being on the ranch alone was frightening. I busied myself with cleaning and organizing and then proceeded to make dinner. It was really too bad Kerrick couldn't come over. As I sat alone, eating a stuffed baked potato, I realized how lonely I was. The house seemed to get bigger by the minute.

Noises came at me from every direction. The wind whistled through the trees sounding like howling wolves in the distance. The slapping of the unlocked barn door against the building was like a hammer beating against a nail. With a headache beginning to surface, I ventured into the dark to lock down the barn.

The sun had set over the mountains, leaving an ominous orange glow. A cool breeze brushed across my neck, making the tiny hairs stand up and a chill run down my spine.

I swore I'd locked the door earlier that day, but with so many things happening at once, I obviously hadn't gotten to it. Sliding the bolt into the slot, I tugged the door, making sure it was closed for the night. Turning around, I saw the dark outline of the cabins, all of them black and barren except the last one. A light burned inside and a shadow crossed the window.

Thump. Thump. Thump. My heart beat against my chest. The shadow loomed in the distance. My eyes never left the cabin. What now? I knew I'd have to face him, but alone? This wasn't how it was supposed to happen. What was I thinking?

A false sense of safety came from his absence. What I didn't see couldn't hurt me. I was stupid to underestimate him. Walking backward, I kept my eye on the cabin. Step by step, I inched my way back toward the main house. I crept up the steps and walked back through the open door, never taking my eyes off the light in cabin number one.

Coldness settled in my body as hands reached around me and roughly grasped my breasts. He painfully squeezed them until he got the response he desired. A cry escaped from the dark recesses of my memories. The familiar, yet terrifying feel of him touching my body sucked the air from my lungs. I tried to catch my breath, but fear had stolen my ability to breathe. Without oxygen, I couldn't fight back.

Breathe.

In.

Out.

Breathe. I was shaking.

Breathe.

Robyn.

Lessons.

Breathe.

What would Robyn say? *Evaluate.* Evaluate the situation. *Come on, Mickey.* Breathe. Talking to myself, I tried to bring calm to my rapidly beating heart. At this pace, I'd pass out, and then what?

Grabbing his hands, I yanked them down and turned to face the last man I'd ever wanted to see. Shoring up my stance, I saw something like smugness reflected in the depth of his eyes. *Jackass.*

"Welcome home, Mickey. How was your vacation?" His eyes danced at my discomfort. I heard Megan's voice warning me, *Play along until you can formulate a different plan.*

"I'm good. Well-rested and ready to start over." *My new life plan didn't have room for this.*

"I'm so happy to hear that. I've missed you. Tell me, what did you learn in prison?"

I learned to survive, asshole. "I had to take anger management classes." I scoured the room trying to find a weapon. Something. Anything. There was nothing. My gun was locked in the safe. Out of reach.

"I hope that you learned how to control your smart mouth. That's always been your problem, you don't think before you speak." He reached up and painfully pinched my lips together. "Your life with me could have gone so much easier if you had just shut your fucking mouth."

Seeing his agitation increase, I changed the subject. I heard Holly tell me to stay true to myself. My beliefs. Right now, I believed I could outsmart him. Right now, I believed I'd do anything to save myself from him.

"Let's not dwell on the past." All I could think about was getting to my phone. If I could just get a message to Kerrick, maybe things would be okay. "I saw the lights on in your cabin. Is there someone with you?" I was hoping against hope he had someone waiting for him. Did I imagine the shadow?

"No one important." He grabbed my elbow and squeezed the sensitive spot on the inside of my arm. I knew his special pinch, it was designed to send me to my knees. "We need to get reacquainted, don't you think?"

I stumbled, trying to keep up with his pace as he dragged me across the living room. My only options were to stay on my feet or be dragged by my arm. He was terrorizing me in the one place I should feel safe—my home.

"Are you hungry? I can make you something to eat. I bought a steak today. I know it's your favorite." *Try to stall him.* I yanked my arm from his and walked to the kitchen, pulled the meat from the refrigerator and set it on the counter. Out of the corner of my eye, I saw my phone next to the sink.

His eyes were on me. Reaching above the sink, I pulled the spices from the cabinet and set them around my phone. When I turned around, he was looking toward the wall that had been spray-painted. Taking advantage of his lack of attention, I quickly slipped my phone into the front of my bra. The problem with dresses was that there was nowhere to hide anything. I prayed he didn't get grabby again.

"I see you didn't like the art. It was my first graffiti job. I thought it was pretty good."

"It wasn't funny." The words 'fucking bitch' screamed through my head.

"It wasn't meant to be funny, Mickey, it was meant to be a reminder to stop being such a bitch." His agitation was growing again. His upper lip curled in a snarl just before he raged. Fear should send me scurrying, but I wasn't that girl anymore. I wouldn't be stupid, but I'd do whatever it took to protect myself.

"Yes, Morgan, you're right. I need to stop being so impulsive." I cringed at the words coming from my mouth—the words that might very well keep me out of the hospital. "I have to go to the bathroom first, and then I'll come and make you dinner. Okay?" I turned away, only to be pulled back. Fear vibrated through my body. *Please, don't find the phone.*

"You haven't given me a kiss yet." He leaned in to press his mouth to mine. Turning away, I avoided the connection.

"Let me brush my teeth first, I just ate onions. I know how you hate them." As quickly as I could, I dashed into the bathroom and locked the door. Pulling out my phone, I typed a message to Kerrick with fingers that shook like a crack addict needing a fix.

HELP! Morgan is here.

"Get the hell out here, Mickey. I'm hungry." His voice was filled with annoyance.

"I'm coming. Let me brush my teeth." I opened the toothpaste and squirted a small dab into my mouth. If I walked out without minty-fresh breath, then all hell would break loose. I put my phone on silent and stuffed it behind the towels in the cabinet. I walked out and directly into his chest. "Were you listening to me? What the hell, Morgan?" I walked past him and straight to the kitchen. All I could do now was stall and hope Kerrick responded. For all I knew, he could be hours away.

"Don't start with me, Mickey. I'm not in the mood. I'm tired and hungry and horny."

"Have a seat, and I'll make you a meal." Mentally crossing my fingers, I prayed he had not changed too much in the past year. "Do you still like it cooked medium-well?" I could take forever to cook his steak if he still liked it cooked to the consistency of shoe leather. I trimmed the fat from the ribeye, sprinkled it with a few spices and tossed it into the hot pan.

"Yep. I'm glad you remembered. Come here and kiss me."

I couldn't kiss him. The thought of him sliding his tongue into my mouth made me want to puke. If I refused him, he'd get angry. That was what got me into trouble before. My refusal always ended up a painful experience.

"Let me finish preparing your dinner." I focused on the sizzling meat. "Besides, we need to talk. I've been gone a year. It's not like I left on good terms." *He couldn't really think I'd want to patch things up, could he?*

"You know I still love you, Mickey. You're forgiven, and we can move forward."

Did he say I was forgiven? Rage flowed through me. Red-hot, angry fury spilled from every pore. "Never once did a punch to the ribs convey the message of I love you." Every ugly word, every bruise, came back to torture me. "A slap to the face doesn't imply you care, Morgan." Turning on my heel, I sprang toward him, not even caring anymore about the consequences. With my hands on his chest, I pushed with all my might and screamed. "You have a fucking crazy way of showing affection."

I knew the slap was coming, but it was worth it knowing I had finally spoken up and was going to put an end to the abuse or die trying.

He hauled back and struck my cheek. The burning sensation fed the inferno of anger roiling inside me. "I told you to watch that smart mouth of yours earlier. You never listen." Grabbing me by the hair, he dragged me toward him and pinned me against the wall. "You'll listen now. I want you to sell the ranch, Mickey. You can't run it, and I want my share." I could feel my hair tear from my scalp.

This wasn't going to end well for me, so I figured I might as well go down fighting. "Fuck off, Morgan, I'm not selling the ranch. It's been in my family for over a century, and I want it for my children and their children."

"Who the fuck would have kids with you?"

I thought about spouting off a list of various men but thought better of it. My cheek was already swelling, and my scalp would be tender for days.

"I leased the land to Tom Morrow. I'm going to open the stables and do boarding. I can make it work." The only reason I was telling him any of this was to stall for time.

His laugh sounded like something out of a horror flick. Its very tone made me shudder, but not in fear. I was tired of being his punching bag. Thankfully, he had eased up on my hair. I made a break for it, but I wasn't fast enough. He cupped the back of my head, pushed me into the kitchen and told me to get his fucking dinner ready as I scrambled toward the stovetop.

"You're leasing the land to that old buzzard? Give me a break, Mickey. You don't have what it takes to make this ranch work."

"No, because you took it all away. Where's the money, Morgan?"

I'd never seen him so angry. The heat coming off him could poach an egg. I said a silent prayer to the universe to please send help. If things continued to escalate, I wasn't going to make it out of this ordeal.

I tried to take things down a notch. "What happened to you? You were so sweet the first six months. The second six months, you became unbearable." I pulled the smoking pan from the heat. Outside, I was the picture of calm; inside, I was fuming, full of pent-up frustration. "I should have told my dad, but he liked you so much, and I didn't want him to be disappointed in you or me. Instead, I allowed you to diminish me with your words and your fists." Saying it made it all the more real. My stupidity was obvious when voiced out loud.

"I'm waiting for my dinner, Mickey. You want to see unbearable? Make me wait just a minute too long. When I'm finished eating, you can spend the night making it up to me. Then we'll talk about the best asking price for the ranch."

I ignored his comment about the ranch. I wasn't selling my family home. I'd find a way to pay him off. "You want your dinner?" My voice hit a pitch that could shatter glass. "Here's your damn dinner."

I tossed the pan with all my might and hit him upside the head. And like the last time I struck him, my aim was perfect. The sizzle of his skin was nothing compared to his scream as the pan seared his cheek. His pain created the distraction I needed. Bolting past him, I ran to the door, flung it open, and hit the firm chest of a police officer.

Morgan's shouts chased me out the door. "You fucking bitch. You'll pay for this."

The officer set me aside and told me to stay put. Several others were scattered across the yard, guns drawn.

Surprisingly, Morgan didn't put up a fight. He stepped outside the house and surrendered. On the driveway, I saw Kerrick moving like a madman toward me.

"Mickey, are you okay?" Collapsing into Kerrick's arms, my tears flowed freely. He picked me up and cradled me in his arms. Tight against his chest, he carried me to the porch where an officer waited. Morgan sat in the squad car with a look of hatred burned into his face.

"Ma'am, I'm Officer Samry. Can you tell me what happened here?"

In a continuous sentence, I spilled out my story. I told him how Morgan came up behind me and accosted me. I explained how I tried to placate him by fixing dinner. I told him how I snuck my phone into the bathroom and texted Kerrick. Finally, I told him how Morgan had slapped me and insinuated about the sexual favors I would owe him. I felt Kerrick stiffen, his posture rigid against my body.

"She would like to press charges against the man." Kerrick's voice was stern and commanding.

"He'll be charged with assault to start with. He'll probably post bail and be out in a day or so. You'll want to make sure you're not alone. He says he lives on the property, which could be problematic. Is there anywhere you can stay?" the officer asked.

"No, I need to stay here. This is my home." Taking in a shaky breath, I eyed Morgan sitting in the back of the police cruiser. His scowl had turned into a cocky *you-can't-hurt-me* expression. I wanted to hit him again with that frying pan.

I signed several forms, and when the last police car drove away, Kerrick and I were left alone. We walked silently into the house.

"I didn't leave the door unlocked all day. I swear. But then I had to leave and lock the barn." Picking up the frying pan and meat off the floor, I cleaned the kitchen. It was a good thing to do when I were stressed. Cleaning was a form of therapy. In a matter of minutes, I could make something that was a mess become orderly again. It was my way to cope.

"Come sit down. I'll clean it up later. Let me put some ice on your cheek, it's red and swollen."

Raising my hand to my cheek, I felt the hot skin where Morgan slapped me. My fear, as well as my defiance, surfaced.

"Why do you look so angry with me?"

His eyes bolted open.

"Christ, I'm not angry at you. I'm furious at myself for leaving you alone." He paced the room, then walked to the freezer to get ice and came to stand beside me. "I should have been here."

"Why should you be here? You have to work. Besides, you have your own life." Taking the towel-wrapped ice from his hand, I brought it to my cheek. I flinched as the cold hit my flaming face. "It's not like you have to babysit me."

"That's exactly what I'm going to do. I'll be working from your kitchen table this week. He's a dangerous man. Just before I received your text, I ran his name through the system." He paced the room again. "He has a history of violence against women. Nothing serious enough to put him in jail for a long time, but enough to show he has a temper that gets away from him."

"That doesn't surprise me. He wants what he wants when he wants it. That's how our problems began. He wanted things from me that I wasn't willing to give him. Mostly sex. It was bad with him. He was selfish and never considered me." The thought of being with Morgan repulsed me.

"Why did you stay with him?" He pulled back the ice and recoiled. It had to look bad for Kerrick to react in that manner.

"That is the question of the day, isn't it?" I stared at the table for a few minutes. "As you may have surmised with your astute detective skills, I was a champion barrel racer. I traveled the United States for years going from competition to competition. I financed the building of the arena and the stables with my winnings." I rose from the table, but he gently pushed me back into my seat.

"Sit. What do you need? I'll get it for you." His tone was gentle and kind.

"A soda, please."

"Continue." He walked to the refrigerator and brought back two cans.

"I wasn't really allowed to date much in high school. Dad was strict. Ranching takes a lot of time, and I was needed here, so there wasn't time for the frivolities of growing up. No weekend movies or days spent at the mall. I was raised as a rancher. Occasionally, I was allowed to go to school events, and of course homecoming and prom. Imagine how I behaved once I was let out of my cage. My dad couldn't go with me to competitions, and he certainly wasn't going to let me go alone, so he hired keepers for me."

"How did you end up with Morgan? He's from Texas."

"Dad came with me to an event in Oklahoma. It was there that he met this amazing roper named Morgan Canter. After some negotiation, Morgan came to Colorado with us. He quickly became part of the M and M ranch family. My dad was like a proud parent. He had two rodeo champions living under his roof."

"How did the romance begin?"

"It wasn't really a romance. We spent a lot of our time together. He showed interest in me, and my dad didn't pull out his shotgun. It was as if I had a green light to date him. I saw it as something good."

"So, your dad picked him out for you." Kerrick's eyes glazed over as his hands squeezed his temples. "What made your dad like him?"

"They were cut from a similar cloth. Both were strong men, both were excellent ranchers, and in the end, both had women who ran from them."

"Did your dad know he was beating you?" The words came out of his mouth in a grumble.

"No, because he wasn't. He was verbally abusive, but most of the men on the ranch talked poorly of and to women. I remember hearing on multiple occasions that women were only good for breeding and feeding. It wasn't until just before my dad died that I felt the first sting of Morgan's slap."

The air in the room sizzled with tension. It was as if my last statement electrically charged the atmosphere.

"Fucking bastard. I want to kill him." His fists slammed against the table, unsettling the half-empty cans of soda. The sound sent me racing from the table. "I'm sorry, Mickey. I didn't mean to scare you. Come back here. I'd never hurt you."

Uncertainty filled me. Could I trust him? He seemed like he was cut from the same cloth as most of the men in my life: strong, powerful, and aggressive. I curled up on the couch and rested my head against the cushion.

"I just want to rest. You don't have to stay here with me. He's in jail for the night. I'll be okay." Curling into a ball, I closed my eyes and tried to relax. Deep down inside I wanted him to stay, but I'd never ask that of him.

"I'm not going anywhere. You've just experienced a traumatic event. You shouldn't be alone. Is there anything I can do to help?"

Alone. That word reminded me that Morgan wasn't alone. I bolted from the couch. "Someone else is on the property. When I was walking back from the barn, I saw a shadow. I thought it was Morgan. That was why I was walking backwards, I didn't want to let him out of my sight. It wasn't him, he was already in the house."

"Stay here and lock the door. Don't let anyone in for any reason. Go get your phone, I'll call you when I want back inside. Do not open the door unless you hear my voice. Got it?"

"Yes." He pulled his weapon from his belt. He disengaged the safety and chambered a round. As soon as he walked out the door, I bolted it shut and ran to the bathroom to get my phone. Curious, I peered out the window and he disappeared into the night.

Biting my nails, I waited an eternity for him to reappear. As soon as I saw his silhouette, I threw the door open and lunged myself at him. With an oomph, he caught me and walked me inside.

"Damn it, Mickey, I told you to wait until I called you. Don't you ever listen?" His harsh voice should have sent me running, but his presence made me feel warm all over.

"Rarely. It's what gets me in so much trouble. I imagine you want to throttle me now, too." I wanted to know who was in the house, but it seemed prudent to let it go for now.

"Yes, I'd like to turn you over my knee, but I'm not that man. Let me run you a bath, and then I'll put you to bed. Since I'll be here a few days, is there a place I can sleep besides the couch?"

"You can sleep with me." The thought of him curled up beside me almost made the ordeal worth living through.

"No, I can't. I don't want to be just another man using you. You've had enough of that in your life."

Shaking my head, I silently cursed myself for my stupidity. He was not my boyfriend, he was a fuck that turned into a friend. He had no interest in me. What did I expect?

"I thought we were using each other?" I pulled my brows together in question.

"I'm sorry about that. I should have listened to my instincts. It won't happen again, I promise."

Stomping toward the bathroom, I pushed the door forward with such force that it came back to nearly knock me out. If it weren't for Kerrick's hand catching the door before it hit me, I'd have been sprawled out on the cold tile floor.

"Leave me be." Ducking under his arm, I moved through the bathroom like an out-of-control storm. My tornado of fury was just waiting to unleash itself.

"What the hell is wrong with you?" His voice was measured but barely controlled.

"What's wrong with me? What's wrong with you? One moment you're all compassion and concern, and the next you're telling me that you're sorry you used me. You're either rushing to be inside of me or rushing to be away from me. What is it, Kerrick?" I turned on the bathwater and pulled a towel from the cabinet. Grabbing the hem of my dress, I pulled it above my head, which left me in nothing but a bra and underwear.

"I'm trying to be a better person, Mickey. I knew right away that you weren't the fuck-and-forget type. I should have listened to my head instead of my dick."

"You know what? You're no different from any of the other men in my life. You demand and push. Some people use their fists to get their way; you use your insensitive, I-don't-give-a-shit attitude to throw the punches for you. You know what, though? Your approach is infinitely more painful."

"Don't you ever compare me to that man. With the exception of the playful swat I gave you on the ass, I've never hit a woman. As for my brusque demeanor, I've never pretended to be anything but what I am. I told you at the grocery store that my expectations are always clear."

"Yes, you did. You expect a whole hell of a lot. I can see why your wife left you. The return on investment for you is poor. Get the hell out of my bathroom." I could tell that my last statement wounded him. Something in his eyes seemed to crack just a little. It was as if I dented his protective armor.

Turning to leave, he stopped at the door and spoke. His voice was measured, his armor resurrected. "There was a woman in his cabin. I sent her packing. If you don't mind, I'll take the spare room next to yours. Goodnight, Mickey." *Why was it that the slap to my face and pull of my hair barely hurt, but the rejection in Kerrick's eyes left me aching?*

Chapter 9

MICKEY

My conversation with Kerrick left me tossing and turning all night. I woke up exhausted. I was not the kind of girl to carelessly fling accusations or snide remarks at someone. I knew how painful words could be. It wasn't my intent to hurt him. I just wanted to shut him up—to stop him from hurting me.

The smell of coffee floated through the air. Sliding out of bed, I freshened up and then lumbered into the kitchen in search of a hot cup of comfort. Kerrick sat at the table in front of his computer.

"Good morning." I approached with shame. My behavior was despicable, and I owed him an apology.

"Good morning. I made coffee. I hope that's okay." His eyes shot to mine and then back to his computer.

"I'm sorry about last night. I really am." The lump in my throat made it almost impossible to finish my sentence. "I'm not like that. I was totally out of line. Can you forgive me?"

"There was nothing to forgive. You were right. I'm bossy and overbearing. I was out of line." I followed his eyes across the room. He appeared to be staring into nothingness. "I hardly know you, and yet I felt somehow I had some say over how things should go with you."

"No, you saved me last night. You held me and cared for me. I lashed out at you because it felt like you were getting ready to toss me aside. You didn't deserve my wrath." Picking up his cup, I walked it into the kitchen to pour my first cup and refill his.

"I wasn't tossing you aside. I was just establishing the expectations. I can't be who you want me to be. You were spot on when you said there would be a lack of return on investment."

The reminder of my words twisted my stomach. Harsh didn't even come close. They sounded fine in the heat of battle, but today they were pure ugliness. "I was wrong, Kerrick. Those were words hurled in anger, not in honesty."

"Let's just move on, Mickey."

With two cups of coffee in my hands, I entered the dining area. Sitting across from him, I noticed the dark circles under his eyes. I guessed he hadn't slept well either.

With my heart squeezing until it hurt, I realized he was the right kind of wrong for me. Strong and dominant, but kind and caring. I'd totally misjudged him. He was nothing like Morgan.

One steaming mug was placed in front of him. "When are you going to bring your horse to the ranch?"

His eyes flew to my face. I wasn't sure if he was shocked by my offer of coffee or the abrupt change in subject.

"I can bring him anytime. What stall do you want me to have?" Back on neutral ground, the conversation flowed smoothly.

"You get first pick of any stall you want." Happy that we were at least talking, I opened the conversation to something a bit more inviting. "I was planning to go to the supply store and pick up feed and other stuff we need for the ranch. I want to make sure everything is ready for your brothers' arrival. Do you want to come with me?"

"Yes. Can you give me half an hour to finish something for work?" His eyes were glued to his computer screen. His fingers tapped rapidly across the keys.

"Of course, but you don't have to come with me. I understand how busy you are."

"I'm coming, Mickey." In spite of our argument, he was sticking around to protect me. That said a lot about him. "Morgan will be released soon. I don't want you anywhere alone until we can figure out a way to get rid of him." He might never have sex with me again, but he was dependable and wouldn't abandon me as his friend. The thought was sobering.

"I appreciate your dedication to my safety. Unfortunately, Morgan will be around for a long time. My dad saw to that." My shoulders slumped as I exhaled. "My dad said as long as there were cattle on the ranch, and Morgan was working here, then he would have a stake in the profits."

Kerrick's eyes widened. Even though I'd only known him a short time, I could see the wheels turning in his head. I wanted to ask him what he was thinking, but he stopped my train of thought with a demand.

"Go get ready. I'll try to wrap this up quickly." His attention became solely focused on whatever it was he was working on.

I rummaged through my closet and located a worn pair of Levis. I'd gained a few pounds in the last few days, but not nearly enough to fill the pants. I couldn't continue to look like a poorly clothed homeless person. Tugging on a tank top and throwing a plaid shirt over it, I spied myself in the mirror. It didn't seem to matter what I put on, I resembled a waif.

Running my fingers through my hair, I pulled my curls back into a ponytail. It felt good to have them off my face. The quick fix to my hair gave me just enough time to put on some makeup before we left. Wasn't it time I paid attention to the details of my life? With five minutes left to spare, I spritzed on my perfume and walked back to the dining area.

Completely zoned into his work, Kerrick was oblivious to my presence. I slid the chair out and sat across from him. As the chair legs creaked against the wooden floor, his eyes flashed up, down, and up again. It was like he was seeing me for the first time.

"Are you almost ready to go?" I asked.

He didn't respond. He stared. Was he staring at me, or through me? It was hard to tell with him. He always had this mask of indifference fixed on his face.

Set Free

"Kerrick?"

"What? Yes, I'm ready. I'll drive." He pushed his chair back, rose, and walked out the door.

I stopped to lock up the house and walked to the side of the truck, where I found Kerrick waiting with my door open. He was a man of contrasts: hard and edgy, and yet soft and caring at just the right moment.

He was so different from Morgan, and yet he was a man. How dissimilar could they be? Resentment flowed through me. I didn't have the luxury to want a man at this point in my life. I took a deep breath and cleared my head of any romantic thoughts I might have had about Detective McKinley.

"WELL, look who the cat dragged in again? After our last meeting, I felt terrible about what Morgan did to you. I had no idea that he shouldn't have been purchasing items on your account," the old man behind the counter said.

I heaved a sigh of weariness. I was so done with Morgan. I just wanted to move on. "It's not your fault. I was careless about the control of the ranch. It's a hard lesson learned, but one that wouldn't have been as clear if not learned the hard way." Turning to Kerrick, I made the necessary introductions. "Mr. Woodruff, this is my friend, Kerrick McKinley. His brothers are coming from Wyoming to help me run the ranch. We are changing what we do. As you have probably heard, we no longer have cattle. We'll be boarding horses, giving riding lessons, breeding and whatever else comes along, so I need to get supplies and feed."

The two men scrutinized each other like they were sizing one another up. Once their silent observation was complete, they offered their hands for a shake and went about their business.

"Can you call your brothers and ask them what type of feed they prefer for their horses? I want them to have what they need when they arrive."

"They can feed their own damn horses. If they want you to feed them, then they can pay you to board them."

"You and I both know that wasn't the agreement. If they're going to work for free, then I need to take care of their needs. Make the call while I grab a few things." Heading off to the clothing section, I left him in silence. It was obvious he was not used to being told what to do. Well, things were going to change. They *had* to change.

Piling my new clothes on the counter, I found Kerrick on the phone. His expression was grim. It was obviously bad news. Perched against the counter, I leaned in and listened for any indication of what the conversation was about. It was not until I heard him say Morgan's name that I realized he was getting information about his release. I waited for him to hang up the phone and clue me in.

"He's being released tomorrow. They suggested you go to the courthouse to apply for a temporary restraining order in the morning. It can be served to him before he exits jail." The reality of Morgan being free again sent a frost through my bones.

"He lives at the ranch. How will that work?" The thought of coming in contact with him again rattled me. What did it take to keep a violent man in jail?

"He has to stay one hundred yards away from you. Failure to keep that distance will send him back to prison."

"All right, I'll go first thing in the morning. Did you get the type of feed your brothers wanted?"

"Yes, I asked Mr. Woodruff to load it into the truck. I hope that's okay." He acted like a boy who'd been caught with his hand in the candy jar. I imagined he felt uneasy doing things on my behalf, especially since our blowout.

"I appreciate your help." I paid the bill and left.

On our way back to the ranch, I enjoyed the scenery. Wide open meadows, wildflowers, blue jays and a sexy, sulking man.

Just before we drove under the sign, I excitedly asked, "When are your brothers going to get here? I'm excited to meet them. In all honesty, I'm eager to have horses on the property again." In spite of everything that had happened, I did look forward to the distraction.

"They will be here the day after tomorrow." He spoke in a soothing voice. "Are you anxious as in enthusiastic, or anxious as in a panic attack is coming?" He pulled the truck up next to the stables so we could unload the feed.

"No, I'm happy. Help me unload this stuff, and I'll tell you my story. It's stupid really. I've had a ton of time to think about it. It all boils down to my impulsivity."

"Big surprise there." He ducked when I tossed a salt lick at him.

We worked side-by-side unloading the truck. I turned and walked to the tack room, hoping he would follow. He did. With my hand gliding over my saddle, I told him my biggest regret.

"The morning my dad died, we had a huge fight. I told him I wasn't sure I wanted to date Morgan anymore. He told me I was fickle and screamed that I was just like my mother. I suppose in many ways, I was like her. I must have been a constant reminder to him. Anyway, Morgan seemed the perfect fit. He was strong and manly, just like I like my men. Unfortunately, that type of man hasn't been good for me." I walked to the wall where row upon row of ribbons hung.

"Go on." He leaned against the saddle horse while I stroked the satin of my last blue ribbon.

"I hated being compared to the woman who had abandoned us, so I got on my horse and took off. I was supposed to ride the fence with him that day. Instead, I was up in the hills licking my wounds while my dad was dying in a field of cow shit." I walked around the room and stopped in front of him.

"You can't blame yourself for your dad's death. You didn't make him have a heart attack." He leaned in toward me. I thought he might pull me into his arms, but he rocked forward and stepped away. I could see in his eyes that he was conflicted about his actions. I disproved his attempt to pardon me.

"I'll never know if I stressed him out so much that he had a heart attack. If I'd been there, would he have lived? I have to live with that forever." It was a huge burden to bear.

"You can't beat yourself up for the rest of your life over it."

"I know that. I did a good job beating myself up that first year. I immediately sold all of my horses, even my prized Mr. Darcy. He was the love of my life. I was out riding him the day my dad died. Somehow, I equated my dad's death with my love of horses. I sold all of them as part of my punishment. I stayed with Morgan as the rest of my sentence. Somehow, I figured if I gave up the one thing I truly loved and stayed with the person I truly loathed, it would be punishment enough. Sadly, I've been punished over and over ever since."

"Stop penalizing yourself." He shook his head and organized the leads that hung on the wall. "I'm glad the horses are coming. I think they'll be a good diversion for you. I'll get Keen as soon as my brothers are here. They can stay with you while I fetch him. I don't want you to be alone."

"I'll be okay. In fact, since I have to go the courthouse tomorrow, why don't you go and get your horse? Surely, I should be safe in the courthouse. Besides, I want to get my hair cut."

"You're not cutting it short, are you?" His abrupt mood change should have caused my head to spin, but I was getting used to him. I imagined it was his way of telling me he preferred my hair long.

Smiling, I replied, "Just a trim and a good conditioning. Is it a deal? You get your horse, I'll get my restraining order."

He chuckled, which I realized now was one of my favorite sounds. *If only he laughed more.* "You drive a hard bargain. Okay, on one condition. You have to text me every time you leave one place and arrive at another. I want to know where you are every minute."

I presented my hand for a handshake that would seal the deal. "I'm hungry. Are you?"

"Starving. Can I take you to lunch?" He didn't wait for an answer. He ran his hand across the small of my back while he guided me to the truck.

"Let's go to Rick's Roost. I've never been there. Is the food good?" I was grateful to get things out in the open. Sharing my story with him had lifted a weight off me that I hadn't known existed.

"It's decent: hamburgers, fries, and stuff, nothing too exciting, but since you started a brawl at Tommy's I think it's the best choice." He put the truck in gear, and we were on our way. It was amazing how fast life could pass you at fifty-five miles an hour.

"Sounds yummy. I'd love a good burger." I licked my lips in anticipation.

"Mr. Darcy, huh? Do you care to discuss why you named your horse Mr. Darcy?" I glanced at him just in time to see his eyes look to the heavens while he shook his head.

"I'm a romantic. I needed a strong man in my life to love me unconditionally. I found him in a horse. He didn't mind my moodiness, and I didn't mind his stubborn streak. When we rode, it was perfect."

"What happened to him?" Pulling into the parking lot, he ran around to open my door.

"Thanks," I said as I hopped out of the truck. "Mr. Darcy was sold to a family near Colorado Springs."

Not much conversation happened during lunch. Both of us were famished and dug into our meals. Full and satisfied, we flagged down the waitress for the check. Kerrick grabbed for it first, but I pulled it from his hand.

"Give it to me," he said. "I always treat my date." He reached over to pull the paper from my fingers.

"I'm not your date. That would require you asking me out and me accepting. Then there would be the real possibility of a relationship, and that's something neither of us is looking for. I'll pay for my meal." I reached into my purse and pulled out a twenty dollar bill. After throwing it on the table, I walked outside and waited for him to catch up.

He seemed to be silently brooding about something all the way home. I didn't wait for him to come around and help me exit. Instead, I hopped out of the truck and went straight into the house. I grabbed a soda from the kitchen, walked into my office and closed the door.

Powering up the computer, I entered the receipts into a spreadsheet and stared at the numbers. Things were going to get grim if I couldn't find an alternative source of income after the snow began to fall.

GETTING a temporary restraining order was easy enough. Morgan getting arrested for assault made it a simple affair. I kept my promise and sent a text to Kerrick at every stop.

My last stop was the beauty parlor. I hadn't had anyone pamper me in a long time. Strong fingers massaged my scalp while I relaxed in the chair. My life paraded through my brain. I had gone along for the ride since I was little. Today, I had taken charge, and it felt amazing. If the ranch made it, it would be my success. If it failed, it would be my failure. It felt good to own my decisions.

"Do you have a date tonight?" the hairdresser asked.

I laughed. "No, I'm not in a relationship with anyone at this point." I wished I could have said yes, but Kerrick wasn't interested, and I didn't have time to waste.

"That's too bad, because you're going to look stunning when I get done with you. Are you sure I can't cut your hair shorter?" *Did I dare cut my hair?* "It would look so nice framing your face."

He was adamant that I leave it long. *This wasn't his choice. This choice belonged to me alone.* I chewed my cheek while I contemplated the change. On a whim, I nodded and sat back to watch the transformation.

A shiver ran through my body as the first snip was made, and several inches fell to the floor. An hour later, I left the salon with a shoulder-length bob. She had blown it dry, and not a curl remained. The style was a dramatic departure from my norm, but nothing could remain the same.

I had been given a second chance, and I planned on doing everything differently. I hopped inside my truck and texted Kerrick.

On my way home. How about fried chicken for dinner? I'll pick it up on my way. Is there any news about Morgan? How is Keen?

M

I turned on the radio and listened to music I'd never heard. It was amazing what I'd missed in the course of a year. I made one last call to the cable company, asking them to flip the switch. Mindless television sounded so good. An incoming text beeped just as I ended the call.

Chicken sounds great. Keen is adjusting to his new home. He loves the window. I wonder how long it will take the little bastard to break free. No sign of Morgan, but he's free. It'll be a few weeks before he gets a court date. Be careful.

K

I will. See you soon.

M

Why was it that I could be arrested and tried in short order and it would take weeks for Morgan to get a court date? There was no justice. I pulled through the drive-thru and picked up dinner. I hated to admit it to myself, but I was looking forward to spending the evening alone with Kerrick. I really hadn't been fair to him. I raged against him, fought with him, and cried a river of tears all over him. He never screamed, never complained, *and* he never hit me. Maybe he was different. I pulled into the driveway, exited the car and turned to admire the sunset.

The sun sat above the mountaintops. Rays of light sliced through the clouds, illuminating the sky with prisms of color. Orange, red, and yellow burst from the peaks. The sight was breathtaking.

"Pretty, isn't it?" His voice scented the air like night-blooming jasmine. Everything about him called to me: his voice, his smell, and his strength. They spoke to me, and I was all ears. How was I supposed to just be his friend?

"It's amazing. I missed this view. My view from prison was the underside of Robyn's bunk. When we were taken outside, the view wasn't much better. The yard was fenced in completely, so you never saw the sun unless it was high in the sky."

"That sounds awful." He looked at me intently. I wondered how long it would take him to notice. "I suppose the only positive thing is you made some good friends in there." He was quicker than most, but maybe that was because he was trained to take notice of everything.

"They're the only girlfriends I've ever had. It's crazy that I had to meet them in prison, right? I wish I could go and see them, but I'm banned from visits. The best I can do is send a letter. They'll want to know how their tequila tasted. Should we go and eat?"

"I'm starved."

"Me, too." I walked past him into the house and straight to the bright kitchen.

"What the hell did you do to your hair?" His voice was commanding but non-threatening. "You said you were just going to trim it." His stance was tall but not aggressive. "It's, like, twelve inches shorter, and where are your curls?" He wanted an answer, but he wouldn't do anything mean to get it.

"My curls are sitting on the floor of the salon." I wondered if he disliked the change. "I needed a change, and I started with my hair." Second-guessing my decision, I questioned if leaving it long and curly would have been a safer choice.

"But you said you were going to get a trim." His hand reached up and stroked my hair. His bright eyes clouded with confusion.

"I did get a trim, it was an extreme trim." Feeling a bit self-conscious, I ran my hand through the soft locks. "Do you hate it?"

He walked around me, silently evaluating my new look. "You look beautiful. It's different, but in a good way. Your eyes somehow have an intensity they were missing before."

"That's the look of determination." I tossed the food onto two plates and took them to the living room.

"It looks sexy on you." Strong fingers ran up the back of my neck and through my hair. I earnestly tried to suppress the moan that his fingers running through my hair pulled from me.

"Let's eat, Detective." I sat in the corner of the couch with my chicken breast, mashed potatoes, and gravy and wondered what in the hell was going on. One moment he was a frigid Fudgesicle, still sweet, but cold and rigid. The next he was warm and comforting… like hot chocolate.

Sliding onto the sofa beside me, he picked up his plate and took a bite of a leg. He must have been starving, because he devoured his meal. His tongue darted out to lick the extra crispy breading that stuck to his lip. It was hard to get the picture of his head between my legs out of my brain.

"Oh, I almost forgot. You said something today that made me think. Our ranch has been in our family for over a century. It goes to the oldest son. My dad would never pass it on to a stranger. He won't split it among the kids, because a fifth of a ranch doesn't hold the value that a full ranch does. We don't own it, but we share in the profits. Your family has owned this ranch for over a hundred years as well. I can't see your dad giving up his family's heritage because he liked or respected a young man."

"What are you getting at?" I sat up and leaned toward him.

"Would you allow me to look at your dad's will? Who interpreted it for you when he died?"

"I read it with Morgan. It said that twenty percent went to him. I was shocked. He seemed shocked as well. You could tell by his expression that he didn't expect it."

"Can I see it later?" He tore into his second piece of chicken and waited for my response. Could there be something I misinterpreted in the will? That would be the best news ever.

"Sure. Before I bring it out, though, I want to meet Keen. I've been excited about his arrival all day."

"Finish eating, and we'll head on out. He would love the company." With his plate in his hand, he walked into the kitchen and cleaned up after himself. I hadn't known many men who did dishes, cleaned, or cooked, but I had seen him do all three, and never once did he make a fuss about it.

Sidling up next to him, I bumped him playfully with my hip, pushing him to the side so I could run my plate under the water. He told me he'd take care of it while I grabbed a sweater. *Unbelievable.*

Before walking out the door, Kerrick took my keys from the table. He guided me out the door and turned around to lock it. Normally I'd have rolled my eyes, but after the other night, I was unwilling to argue his valid points.

It was dark in the country, no streetlights to dim the stars, nothing to illuminate the path. A chill ran through me as I relived the frightening night with Morgan. Kerrick must have had a sixth sense. He reached down and took my hand in his, offering comfort.

"I've got you. He won't ever get near you again. I promise." He pulled me to his side. His hand slid up my arm and rested on my shoulder in a buddy sort of way.

Keen stirred as we approached the barn. I flicked the switch and listened as the light crackled to life. Keen leaned his head over the gate and snorted. He was a beautiful bay, his auburn coat shined like he was dipped in copper. This was a horse that had been loved.

"He's beautiful, Kerrick." I walked slowly to his pen. Reaching up, I stroked his mane. He pressed his muzzle forward across my shoulder and into my hair.

"He seems to like your hair."

I noticed how Kerrick caressed Keen's cheek. Every motion was deliberate, soft, and caring. This was a man who took care of what belonged to him. Oh, to belong to a man like him.

Gripping the horse's muzzle, I pulled him toward me and breathed into his nostrils before I whispered to him. My voice was barely audible. "You are one sexy man, just like your owner. You're big and strong, and I bet you give an excellent ride."

"What are you saying to my horse?" He leaned in to brush his lips against Keen's muzzle. If there was ever a time to envy a horse, this was it.

"I'm just getting acquainted. He seems to like having sweet nothings blown in his ear. What about you? When you dated, did you like your girlfriend to whisper in your ear?"

"I don't think I've had someone whisper in my ear." He leaned against the door and watched me. "Do you want to be the first?"

"You said you don't want a relationship, and yet you've been flirting with me all day. What's the deal, Kerrick? You have my head spinning. You make my womanly parts flutter when you're near. Just when I think you might want me, you change your mind." I stretched to bring my lips to his ear and whispered, "Do you want me?"

"God, yes, I want you, but I'm not good for you. Despite knowing that, I can't get you out of my head. When I breathe, I taste you. When I close my eyes, I see you lying naked beneath me. Don't ever think it's because I don't want you. I've had you, and it will never be enough."

"Why can't you just go with it? Stop being so noble." The horse fussed as my voice rose.

"I'm not relationship material, Mickey. I don't want to be the next man to disappoint you. I know I'd hurt you, and you don't deserve that."

Shit. *I* was becoming all too familiar with the look on his face and the tone of his voice. It was the one that said he intended to get his way. He was turning me down—again. I had been bullied and bulldozed my entire life by the men who had claimed to love me. This man in front of me said he wanted me, but it wasn't enough. Bullshit! He needed to know he was good enough and he was a more than fine specimen of a man. Everything about him appealed to me. He needed to know his value. *Even if he didn't want me, he needed to know he was worthy of being loved. Everyone was.*

I pulled him away from the stall so we didn't upset the horse. "Kerrick, you're a great guy, but you're a hypocrite." Taking his hand, I pulled him to the door. "You tell me that I can't beat myself up over the past, but here you are clubbing yourself over the head on a regular basis. Your ex-wife was a twat for telling you that you aren't relationship material. You weren't relationship material for her." Shutting off the light in the stables, I closed the door and stood in front of him. "It wasn't that you weren't enough for her, it was that she was confused on what she wanted. I'm not confused. I've had shit for boyfriends, so even at your worst, you're an upgrade. I'm not begging you to like me, I just wanted to set the record straight." Taking his hand, I guided him into the house for the night. I spent it watching mindless television. He spent it watching me.

Chapter 10

MICKEY

The shrill of my cell broke the silence of the morning. Scrambling from my bed, I reached for the phone. Who would be calling me this early? I recognized the number as Dr. Mallory's.

"Hello," I croaked out. My whisper of a voice was an obvious sign that I had just woken up.

"Good morning, Mickey. Sorry to call you so early, but I have a bit of an emergency. As you know, several horses remain homeless due to the fires in the Pikes Peak region. I got a call today, asking me if I could find a home for two of them. They're healthy but spirited, and the current guardian is finding them difficult to manage. They don't have the land or facilities that you have. Are you interested?"

I shook my head to break out of the morning stupor I was in. Did he just offer me two unruly horses? I suppose the best way to see if my new help were good with horses would be to challenge them.

"How old are these horses?" I don't want to bring a horse on board that had a foot in the grave. I wouldn't mind being the final home to retired equine, but at this point I couldn't afford their care. Anything that came to this ranch had to pull its weight.

"Brandy is six, and Sir D is eight. I've seen them, and they're beautiful. Sir D is more spirited, but I think he's bored. He used to be a competition horse, and now he's left out to pasture. He needs a challenge. What do you say? I'll pick them up and bring them to you."

I weighed the pros and cons in my head. Free young horses were exactly what I needed. I couldn't claim to own a horse ranch without horses. Besides, it would keep my new help busy.

"I'll take them. My new ranch hands are arriving with their animals today. When do you want to bring the orphans?" I giggled to myself. It would appear that the ranch was turning into some kind of refuge, a second-chance ranch for everyone.

"How about I bring them tomorrow? In exchange for taking the horses in, I'll look over your animals to make sure they're healthy. Traveling is very stressful on animals."

"That would be great. What time should I expect you?" Things were beginning to get busy, so having a time would help me prepare for my day. With animals beginning to fill the stables, early mornings would become the norm.

"I should be there around noon or shortly thereafter. Thanks, Mickey. You're a horse saver."

Disconnecting the call, I rolled out of bed and walked toward the kitchen. Sitting shirtless at the table was Kerrick. His eyes were trained on his computer. The coffee was ready, my cup was set out in front of the pot. The simple gesture warmed my heart. He was thinking about me while I was sleeping.

"Good morning, Sugar. How did you sleep?"

Addressing me in such a sweet, endearing manner made me melt. It was nice to have someone call me something other than bitch. The problem was that endearments were meant for lovers or partners, and we were neither.

"I slept well until my phone went off this morning." I was excited about taking in the strays.

"What was the call about?"

"Horses. Roland is bringing two rescues."

"That's great. This place is turning into an actual horse ranch."

My eyes scanned his naked chest. His chest was great, the horses were only nice. I lowered my gaze but found it hard to take my eyes completely off his well-developed muscles. I stared at his long torso and narrow waist. A waist that connected to powerful thrusting hips that…

My thoughts were interrupted by his laughter.

"If you're hungry, I can get you something to eat. You don't have to stare at me like a starving woman."

"Asshole." I retreated into my bedroom to get ready for the day. I had a horse to tend to and a ranch to run.

Re-emerging thirty minutes later, I was dressed in my new perfectly fitted jeans. My hair fell softly on my shoulders, and the touch of makeup I'd put on made me feel pretty.

I found him still at his computer, only this time he was fully clothed. Our eyes met as I made my way back to the kitchen. I swore I could see a flash of amusement in them. The man was a sadist. He was obviously getting some kind of enjoyment from my discomfort. Well, two could play at his game. I wondered how hungry he'd get if I decided to dish up my brand of temptation. Game on.

With a peach in my hand, I leaned over him to grab a napkin from the center of the table. Sure, I could walk to the other side and pick one up just as easily, but it wouldn't be as effective. Rubbing my breasts against his back as I reached for the paper was exactly what I'd intended to do. If his stiff reaction was any indication, then I had hit the exact mark I was targeting.

Sitting next to him, I stared until he gave in and glanced in my direction. At that moment, I bit into the juicy flesh of the fruit and let the nectar run down my chin. Rather than use the napkin to mop it up, I ran my tongue past my lips and across my chin to sweep up the sweetness. His eyes never left my tongue. If I were a betting woman, I would imagine he might be thinking about the things I'd done to him with that very same tongue, just days ago.

"I'm getting horses tomorrow. Two rescues are coming our way. I'm going to have to set up an account so your brothers can purchase supplies. Are they trustworthy?"

He said nothing, only stared at my mouth.

"Kerrick, are you listening? I asked if your brothers were trustworthy."

"What?" He ran his hands over his eyes. "Of course they are. They're McKinleys. We may be horse thieves, but we're not criminals." His lip twitched as he tried to keep a straight face. "You can trust my brothers, but it would probably be a good idea to put a maximum purchase amount on any account. After what happened to you, I'd be very wary of anyone regardless of their references."

"That's very good advice, Detective. Thanks for the insight. I'm off to take care of your horse. Is there anything you need?"

He took me in while he bit his lip. I'd watched him for days; the way he bit his lower lip was a telltale sign of attraction. He seemed to bite it every time he saw something he liked or wanted. It had happened both times we had sex. He did it when I stripped in front of him in the bathroom. He chewed his lip as I walked in front of him this morning in my nightshirt and morning hair. He could push me away, but he couldn't deny he wanted me. That bit of information was powerful.

"Can I look at the will? You were going to get it for me last night, but you didn't."

"Sure." I walked to my room to retrieve the will from the safe and handed it to him on my way out the door.

"HEY, HANDSOME." I hooked up the lead and walked Keen into the paddock. I talked to the horse for a few minutes and then released him to run around. He bolted from me and ran in a circle along the fence. There was no greater joy than to see a horse run free. His mane flowed in the breeze, and his tail whipped around like a flag.

Heading into the stalls, I cleaned his. It didn't take long. I poured a bit of grain in his bin and tossed in an apple and a carrot for a treat.

I knew the minute Kerrick walked into the stables, I felt him.

His presence seemed to permeate the room, no matter how large the space. The air seemed thinner when he was near, it was like he sucked the oxygen right out of the room. I inhaled a large amount of air trying to fill my lungs, knowing that within minutes it would all be gone.

Why I reacted to him so strongly, I didn't understand. He was very clear about his intentions, he had none concerning me. He was attracted to me but not enough to let go of the notion that he was a bad bet. I wanted to kick myself for telling him he would be a bad return on investment. I'd spoken from a place of anger, not from a place of truth.

"What are you doing lurking in the stables? When I left you, you were working on something else."

"I'm taking a break." He reached for the shovel and tossed a few shovelfuls of wood pellets on the floor. "Why do you use the pellets? Aren't they more expensive?" Rather than put the shovel back, he leaned it against the wall and bent over to pick up a few of the pellets in his hand.

"Initially, it's more expensive. However, it cleans up easier and requires less over time, so it evens out. Grab the hose and give the new pellets a misting. They will fluff up and Keen will like their softness. I'm going to fill his haynet." I felt his eyes on me. A giddy feeling took over as I walked away. I might look like I had a skinny ass in my baggy pants, but in my new jeans my butt looked fabulous.

When I returned, I found Kerrick in the paddock with his horse. Standing in the shadow, I watched them play. A game of tag seemed impossible, but seeing it with my eyes made me a believer. The way he touched his horse was funny. He tapped, and the horse ran. The horse nudged, and Kerrick chased. That man and his horse had a connection. Laughing out loud, I caught myself and cussed. *Shit.* Our eyes met. The moment was gone. He knew I was watching.

With his long gait, it took seconds for him to appear at my side.

"Are you finished?"

"What? No. I'm taking a break. I have eight stalls to get ready, six for your brothers and two for tomorrow's arrivals." Behind him, Keen appeared to be waiting for his owner to come back and play. "Do you want him to stay in the paddock for a while, or do you want him back in the stable?" I mentally slapped myself upside the head. "Will Houdini jump the fence?" Leaving the horse alone was risky. Kerrick had already told me he was an escape artist.

"No, he breaks out to get to open space. Once he's in open space, he won't leave. Can you give me a few minutes? I went over the will, and I think you need to read something again." He didn't wait for my answer. He expected compliance. I didn't question him. I followed.

In the kitchen, he pulled out my chair. Always the gentleman, he situated me first, and then pulled over a seat to sit beside me. The will sat in front of me. He had highlighted several lines.

Morgan Canter is entitled to twenty percent equity of the cattle ranch. The following conditions apply.

The ranch must remain in good standing.

The aforementioned foreman must help to maintain the ranch's value.

Herd numbers must steadily increase to meet the goal of eighteen hundred.

Looking over the list, I saw it. The bastard had broken every rule set out for him. I never questioned the word 'equity'. I took it to mean ownership, and so did Morgan. We were stupid. In reality, it meant his share of earnings, provided he produced. The stupid asshole fucked himself over. He sold himself out. By selling the cattle, he put the ranch in jeopardy, ruined any hope of building equity, and destroyed the prerequisite to increasing the herd. His greed was his undoing.

Grabbing Kerrick by the collar, I pulled his mouth to mine. I didn't care if he didn't want to kiss me. I was kissing him. His ability to extract information from a simple conversation would rid me of Morgan for good. My world would be brighter because he saw and heard everything. Not once did I admire that trait until now. Perception often changed when reality was clear.

Sparks flew as soon as our lips met. The attraction was obvious. Tongues tangled. Hands dragged through hair. Moans escaped. He lifted me from my bottom as I wrapped my legs around him. The journey to my room began.

"Bad Boys" rang from his phone. The minute the song came on, I knew our trip to the bedroom had been canceled. Disappointed, I slid down his body and walked out the front door. Confusion littered my mind. We'd almost made it to my bed despite his attempts to avoid a sexual relationship with me. My body quaked with pent-up desire. I needed to ease the sexual tension pulsing between my legs. I walked to the stables to complete my unfinished chores, hoping I could sweat my horniness away.

The crunching of tires on gravel drew my attention to the outside. I'd finished with the stalls and had cleaned and oiled the saddles in the tack room.

Men's voices carried across the field. Hidden behind the door, I peeked out to watch three men embrace. Kerrick's brothers had arrived. Laughter filled the air, the breeze carried their voices. All three men stood with their bodies toward me. They couldn't possibly see me peeking from behind the door, could they? They had the same brown hair and build. All three were muscular, with nary an ounce of fat on them. Kerrick pointed in my direction. The two new arrivals hopped into their trucks and drove forward.

Not wanting to get caught eavesdropping, I hightailed it to the tack room and tried to look busy. It would be so easy to hide all day, but I couldn't; I had a ranch to run and cowboys to meet.

"Hi, you must be Keagan and Killian. I'm Mickey." Smiling wide, I took in the sight of the three men standing before me. I tried to appear confident in spite of the doubt that threatened to consume me.

"Yes, but do you know who's who?" The man on the left raised a brow in question. His stance was wide, like he just got off his horse rather than out of his truck. Both men wore cowboy hats and boots. If I didn't know better, the men could be triplets. All Kerrick needed was a Stetson, and they would be impossible to tell apart.

"No, I have no idea who's who. I know Kerrick, but you two have me stumped." I pushed the stray hairs that had fallen in my face aside. I wanted to figure out how to tell the three apart. On closer inspection, I saw that only Kerrick had brown eyes. One brother had blue/green hazel eyes, and the quiet brother had blue. The man to the right still hadn't said a word.

"Let's put you out of your misery. This here is Keagan." Kerrick pointed to the man on the left. Which meant the silent one was Killian. "This is Killian."

I could sense the pride Kerrick felt toward his brothers.

"Welcome to M and M ranch. I'm so excited to have you here. Let me show you the stables. Once we get the animals settled, I'll show you your houses. They do come furnished, but you're welcome to replace or change anything. They have the essentials."

I showed them the stables and where I expected them to house their horses for now. When the stables filled up, I'd have them take their animals to the staff stables behind the cabins. Until then, it didn't make sense to house them in two different places.

Keagan was the first to speak. "We're happy to be here, ma'am. It will be nice to have the freedom to do some things on our own."

"I'm happy to have you. I thought if you weren't too tired from the drive, I'd take us out for dinner and a drink. If you're not up to it, then I'll have something delivered to the house. The main house has an open door policy. Well, it used to be until your brother came along, but you're welcome to come hang out any time you please."

Kerrick didn't seem pleased with my statement. Was it because I outed him for his controlling security demands, or because he didn't want his brothers hanging out with me? *Interesting.* "I'll leave you to get situated. Let's meet up at the main house at six. If you're up to it, we'll go to Rick's Roost. They have great burgers."

AT PRECISELY SIX O'CLOCK, the three brothers showed up on my doorstep. Keagan and Killian looked tired, and Kerrick seemed more relaxed than I'd ever seen him. We piled into my truck and headed into town. At Rick's Roost, I ordered their food and placed a pitcher of beer on the table.

"So tell me," Keagan asked, "how did you meet my brother?" I looked from brother to brother before I answered. I wanted to see if Kerrick was giving me some kind of silent warning. I saw nothing in his expression.

"Yeah, Mickey, how did we meet?" Playful Kerrick was present, and he was egging me on.

"Your brother picked me up on the side of the road." I waited to see if he'd elaborate, or if he would let me get away with my abbreviated answer. He said nothing.

Killian spoke for the first time. "Why were you on the side of the road?" His Barry White-deep voice surprised me.

"I had no ride." The men sat in silence for a few minutes. Kerrick was grinning, Keagan was drinking his beer, and Killian seemed to be contemplating.

"Why didn't you have a ride? You own a truck, right?"

He just wouldn't let it go. I blurted out, "I'd just gotten released from prison. There, are you satisfied? Boy, you McKinleys are relentless when it comes to extracting information. What's the deal with you three?" The question floated in the air for several seconds before the three of them broke out into raucous laughter. "What's so freaking funny?"

"We already knew your story. We just wanted to see if you would own it, and you did. Good for you. We don't care that our boss is an ex-convict; we just want to make sure that you don't go to jail again, or else we'll be homeless and unemployed. Once you leave the family ranch, it's expected you only return for the holidays." Keagan lifted his glass in salute. "Here's to second chances." We raised our glasses in return, and a hear-hear could be heard throughout the restaurant. The McKinley boys were loud.

After the meals were eaten, Killian eyed his brother and asked, "Are you two a couple? I see the way you look at her, and I swear it's the look of possession." A smug look spread across his brother's face. "You didn't say anything about dating my new boss. You said you were protecting her."

Kerrick paused and glanced around the table. I was caught breathless by his look. He pinned me with a look of ownership. His eyes bore deep into my being. I imagined for just a moment that he would claim me in front of his brothers. Did the unfinished business from this afternoon change his mind? Did he choose to investigate where a relationship with me could go? I waited for his answer with baited breath.

"Nope, we're not a couple. She's available and willing." He gave me an impassive look and proceeded to drink his beer.

I swallowed the lump in my throat. I willed the tears that threatened to spill to recede. He had rebuffed me for the last time. How dare he tell his brothers that I was available *and* willing? Who was he, my pimp?

"Fabulous. Then I can ask her to dance without getting my ass kicked." Keagan jumped off the stool and pulled me with him. "My brother's full of shit. He obviously likes you." He took me to the dance floor, where several people were moving to another song I didn't recognize. "Don't give up on him. He's wounded, and his scars will take time to heal."

"I have no idea what you're talking about." Even his brother saw the attraction between us. I rocked back and forth to the rhythm of the music and ignored any talk of relationships. *What could have been never would be.*

"Who are you trying to convince, yourself or me? I'm just telling you what I see. I think I'm qualified to observe. I've been looking up to him for twenty-eight years."

"Keagan, I think he believes what he says, regardless of what you think. He's made it clear he doesn't want me."

He shook his head and mumbled, "McKinley men are stubborn and dense."

Once the dance was over, I paid the tab and we headed back to the ranch. The dark cabins indicated Morgan was still missing. At the house, we said our goodbyes. Keagan and Killian made their way to the cabins while Kerrick and I walked into the main house.

"Mickey, can we talk for a few minutes?" He walked to the table and sat down.

"I get it, you don't have to beat a lame horse. We're not a couple, we had sex, it was nice, and it's over. Let's move on. I don't want to hear about it anymore. Okay?" I couldn't listen to him dismiss what happened between us any longer. Not feeling the same as he did, each time he simplified our union cut me deep. I went into it knowing it was just sex, but when I came out, it seemed like something more. Chalk it up to a year in prison. My ability to filter things was skewed. Leave it to me to fall for the first man I saw. *What an idiot.*

"I was just going to suggest that you get a lawyer to draft up a letter to Morgan. He should also be served with an eviction notice. The faster you get him off the property, the better. Where do you think he's staying?"

Oh, God. I felt like an idiot. I was talking about our non-relationship, and he was talking about evicting Morgan. "Oh, you're right. I'll call my dad's lawyer tomorrow to clarify things. Now that your brothers are here, there's no need for you to stay. I'd like you to go." The look of hurt washed over his face, but his non-expressive façade quickly replaced it. "I appreciate all that you have done for me. Boarding for Keen will be on the house this month. It's my way of saying thanks."

"Mickey, I want to pay you for Keen. I was also going to ask if you would consider renting one of the cabins to me." *Rent a cabin to him?* "I'd like to be close to my brothers." Would I be able to live on the same property as him without constantly longing for him? I considered his request and decided that whether it was him or his brothers, the fact that the McKinley boys looked nearly identical would be a constant reminder regardless.

"You can take cabin number six. Your brothers are in seven and eight. I haven't the foggiest idea what to charge you for rent, so whatever you think is fair is fine with me."

"I can pay eleven hundred right now. If that's okay with you, then we'll call it that." He watched me like a hawk watches prey. "What about utilities?" Was he trying to see my reaction to him living on the property, or was he looking for something else?

"Almost everything is solar. We also use propane, but I'll take care of that. We are on a well system, so there are no current costs associated with water. Internet and phone are at your expense. You're welcome to log onto my Internet account, but I'm not sure how strong the signal will be in your cabin." The conversation continued as if we were landlord and tenant. I handed him the key to the cabin and walked him to the door. The ranch had four people living in it. By all accounts, I should feel settled. The future was looking positive. I was my own boss and now had ranch hands that reported to me. Yet, I'd never felt so alone.

Chapter 11

MICKEY

In the barn at five in the morning, I had sentenced myself to a lifetime of early wake-ups by bringing horses back to the ranch. I rounded the corner and found the McKinley boys were already hard at work. Keen had been led out to the pasture. His stall was clean and ready for his return.

"Glad you could sleep in," Keagan said while he cleaned out one of the stalls. Next to him was quiet Killian, brushing the coat of a beautiful chestnut mare.

"Sleep in?" My tone was that of disbelief. "It's five o'clock in the morning. What time do you start?" There was absolutely no reason to get out here before five.

"We started at four-thirty. Killian wanted to get the horses settled and inventory the gear." He finished with the stall and moved on to pet the chestnut mare.

"What's her name? She's a beauty." The muzzle of the horse felt soft under my fingertips.

"Her name is Breeze. If we can get her acclimated to her new environment, she's going to enjoy some time with our super stud, Brody. He'll be servicing all the girls we brought from Wyoming." He ran his hand down her mane. "If luck will have it, we should be expecting four foals next summer. What do you think of that?" Four foals by next summer would be amazing. It would be a lot of work, but it would be astounding.

"Really? How will this work for us, Keagan? These are your horses. How will they benefit and bring profits to the ranch?" The financial affairs of the ranch were my number one priority.

"The horses belong to Killian and me, but their offspring belong to the ranch. We need to discuss the details of how Killian and I can earn our keep and our livelihood, but first we need to impregnate these mares. We brought two stallions. They're in high demand, and I've already set up some servicing appointments. Brody is booked until the end of foaling season. Diesel still has a few openings. They are both world-class stallions and get $1200 for insemination services. All six horses have American Quarter Horse Association pedigrees and champion American Cutting Horse Association records."

"That's impressive. How many of these stud appointments are we housing? I need to know to get the stalls ready. Also, the vet is coming today to look at the horses. He wants to make sure they fared well on the trip." Roland should be pulling up sometime after lunch. Excited about the new horses coming in, I walked forward to meet the ones that had arrived.

"I imagine we will have at least ten stalls filled until the end of foaling season, which is October. Both Brody and Diesel can cover a mare up to seven times a day. I wouldn't put them under that much pressure, but I've seen them do it." I thought about the two stallions and all of the sex they'd be having. *Lucky bastards!* At least someone or something would be getting sex. Lord knew it wouldn't be me.

I walked through the stable and met the other horses. Sunset, Magic, and River all came to greet me. Their official names began with McKinley's. McKinley's Sunset was my favorite by far. She sported an auburn coat and symmetrical white socks on all four legs. She was a beauty.

"I'm heading to the store to get stuff for lunch. Do you need anything?" I walked out the door.

"Wait up. You can't go alone. Kerrick says it's not safe for you.

One of us will join you." Great, it was bad enough with one bodyguard, now I had three. "One of us will meet you by the truck in fifteen minutes."

I walked into the house to freshen up, and fifteen minutes later I saw Kerrick leaning on my truck. It would appear that I would have the same protector as always.

I stomped to my truck with determination. "Don't you have a job? I thought you were married to your work." He jumped into the passenger side before I revved the engine and drove down the gravel path.

"I'm on vacation for two weeks. I need the time to move and since my brothers just arrived, I thought I'd take the time to help them get adjusted to Colorado. My most recent investigation is complete, so the timing is perfect." He leaned back after buckling himself in and sighed. He seemed pretty pleased with himself.

"It's not like they moved here from New York. They come from one state away." God, was he really going to be around nonstop for weeks?

"No, but the whole experience is a change for them. They are adjusting to a new home, a new ranch, and you."

Adjusting to me? How hard could it be to live on my ranch? I thought about all of the unknowns we were facing and decided it was best to call a staff meeting tonight. We needed to iron out the details. The men needed to know what they had to gain from being here, and I needed to know how to prepare.

We arrived at the store and loaded up the cart with snacks, fruit, and cold cuts for several days of lunches. Of course, the cashier had to be the same nasty piece of work from before.

"Hey, you two are back. I have to say, you make the cutest couple." She flashed her whitening strip smile at us.

Getting ready to correct her assumption, I said, "Oh, we're—"

"We're incredibly happy together." Kerrick finished my sentence and pulled me to his side. His lips brushed against my temple as his hand rubbed across my back. *What the hell?* The man was going to give me a case of whiplash. He had my head shifting in so many directions, I couldn't be sure where I stood anymore.

We loaded up the groceries and headed home. Once in the car, I turned on him like an angry animal.

"What the hell are you doing? We're not a couple. You made that clear from the get-go. I don't need a bodyguard anymore. What good were you doing sitting in the house anyway? Morgan could have cornered me in the stables, and you would have never known it. Your brothers are around, and I plan on bringing in more help as soon as the stalls are full." The tension in my jaw made my teeth hurt. This man drove me crazy, and not in a good tingly way.

"Contrary to what you believe, I've watched you like a hawk. I knew every time you took a step outside the stables. I checked on you, and you never once caught me. That's why you need me. You don't pay attention, and you're careless when it comes to your safety. I bet the house is unlocked."

Shit, did I lock the house or not? "I'm watching out for Morgan. I have a few ideas about where he's staying. He has horses. So they must be somewhere, and I think he's probably at the Circle C Ranch. They are the only folks around here who might take him in. I'm not an idiot." Circle C was less of a ranch and more of a commune. It was a drifter's location.

"No one said you weren't looking out for him. By the way, the cashier is the girl I tossed out of Morgan's cabin the other night. I didn't want her to know that we aren't a couple. She is a direct link to Morgan."

"You should have told me. That lying bitch said she hadn't seen him, and she was at his cabin that night? She said he split her lip, and she never wanted to see him again." Why did so many women overlook that kind of behavior?

"He's dangerous, and when he finds out you're going to evict him completely from your life, he's going to retaliate. I don't want you to face him alone."

"You're right." The thought of retaliation from Morgan silenced me. He was capable of just about anything. "You've been right about everything. I don't feel safe at night by myself. The main house is the first building you hit on your way into the property. What's to stop him from breaking in in the middle of the night?"

Left with few options, Morgan could become deadly. A cold stillness settled in my bones.

"Nothing, but you kicked me out last night. Do you have any idea how hard it was to leave you alone?"

I wondered if he had any idea how hard it was to *be* alone?

"I appreciate your concern. I can't expect you to protect me, but I have no other ideas." God, please let him suggest that he move back in.

"I can move back in until the situation with Morgan is resolved, if you want me to do that."

Yes. "If it's not too much trouble, I'd be grateful to have your protection." I controlled my excitement by focusing on the road ahead. "In lieu of payment, can I board your horse for free?" Inside, I was doing a happy dance. Kicking him out of the house was impulsive and stupid. When would I learn?

"No, Mickey. I'm doing it because I'm your friend. I don't expect anything in return." We pulled up to the house and unpacked the groceries. Kerrick left to get some of his belongings. The remaining two McKinley men were left on guard. The next hour was filled with phone calls, one to an attorney to draw up Morgan's eviction notice and outline the conditions of my dad's will. The other was to the farrier to schedule monthly appointments to shoe the horses.

The grinding of tires on gravel alerted me to someone's arrival. It was either Kerrick or Roland. Both made my heart beat faster. Kerrick because, well…he was Kerrick and Roland…because he was bringing two horses. Peeking out the front window, I deduced it was Roland. Kerrick wouldn't be pulling a horse trailer.

Excited, I raced to help with the two horses. Roland was exiting the truck as Keagan and Killian walked toward the side of the trailer. One of the men threw the latch, and the excitement began. Coaxing the horses out, Keagan placed the harness over the black horse, and she obediently followed him. She had a perfect white diamond on her forehead and two white socks on her front legs. Keagan walked the mare to Killian, who settled her down with a low murmur and a soft touch. The other horse was being more difficult. He didn't want to back out of the trailer. He was the exact color of Mr. Darcy and had the temperament to match.

I'd been stupid to give up my horses. I hadn't been thinking, only feeling the sorrow that came with losing my father. Morgan had been standing above me, telling me that cattle ranching was now my life, and the horses would only be a hobby. There would be no more rodeos, no more travel.

His message combined with the guilt I felt finalized my decision. The horses were gone within a week. The horses were everything, and I tossed them aside like they had no value. One of the things I valued most was loyalty. Where was my loyalty to my horses?

Keagan threw the rope over the large horse's head and guided him backward with care. Inch by inch, he came into view. I fell to my knees when the horse turned toward me. There was no mistaking the spirited mount. Mr. Darcy had come home.

All three men stood in the center of the yard, confused. The only two beings that knew what was going on were the horse and me, and neither of us was talking. I sat in a heap on the dirt as the horse struggled to free himself. Loosening the lead, Keagan allowed the horse some room. In a few strides, the sorrel lurched forward and stood beside me. His muzzle pushed at my hair. With a bit more force, the big horse pushed against me and knocked me over. Lying on the ground, I laughed and cried. All three men stood with wide eyes and curious looks.

Grabbing the horse, I planted a soft kiss on his forehead. Scrambling to my feet, I walked around him to inspect his condition.

"Mickey, do you care to fill us in? Do you know Sir D?"

Through tears of joy, I spoke. "Gentlemen, I'd like you to meet Mr. Darcy, the love of my life. I gave him away after my father died, and I never thought I'd see him again. What are the chances he would show up here?" I ran my hand across his soft coat, inspecting every inch of him. He was exactly as I remembered him to be. Perfect.

"You're shitting me?" Keagan shouted. "This is your horse from years ago, and he just shows up on your doorstep as a rescue? No fucking way."

"Language," Roland said, looking toward Keagan.

"Sorry, I wasn't thinking. Mickey lives on a ranch. I assume she's heard swear words before today. I didn't mean to offend you, Doc." Keagan tried to pull the horse from Mickey's side, but the gelding wouldn't budge.

"Don't worry about my sensibilities. I cuss all the time. Nothing that comes out of your mouth will make me blush," I said to Keagan. "I'll take care of him."

Pulling Mr. Darcy toward the stables, I turned back and addressed the three men. "Keagan, show Dr. Mallory to your horses. Killian, please take Brandy into the stables and get her settled into a stall. Mr. Darcy and I have some catching up to do."

I took the halter from Keagan and led the big horse to the paddock. He followed me obediently. I walked next to Mr. Darcy and spilled my heart out to him. I apologized for the last few years and promised to give him a good life. He whinnied and lowered his head to me. My heart felt full, which made me realize how empty it had been without him.

I fed him, brushed him, walked him, and whispered my love to him.

My grumbling stomach reminded me that I owed the men lunch. Leading Mr. Darcy to pasture, I released the lead and he galloped free. His mane blew in the air as he ran. Who would have thought I'd get a second chance to make it right with him? Life was full of surprises.

Turning around, I ran smack into Kerrick. *How long had he been standing there?*

"Beautiful horse you have there. My brothers told me what happened. I'm speechless." He placed his arm around my shoulder and pulled me in for a friendly hug. "Do you want to take him out for a ride later? It would be best if someone were with you just in case he's picked up some bad habits. I've been dying to take Keen on the trails. What do you say?"

"I have to make lunch for everyone." I broke free of his hold and headed for the house. "After lunch, I'd love to go for a ride."

I laid out enough food for an army. Kerrick phoned his brothers and told them to come to the main house. The three men walked in talking about horses. Even Killian was taking part in the conversation. He had plenty to say when someone was talking about something that interested him. Bits and pieces of the conversation led me to think another expensive trip to the supply store was in my future.

"Roland, how do the horses look?" Going from zero horses to eight in two days was overwhelming. Making sure the horses were healthy was the first step to calming me.

"I checked out Brandy and Sir...I mean Mr. Darcy before I transported them, and they are in great shape. Mr. Darcy seems happy. He's not a difficult horse with the right trainer. He was obviously missing you. As you know, horses have memories like elephants, they never forget a person, whether they were good to them or bad. The other six are in excellent shape. You've hired some fine horsemen, Mickey. I'm proud to refer their services to my clients. Also, I think we can have the stalls filled in the next few months, if that's what you want."

"I need to have them filled with paying clients if I have any hope of keeping the ranch." We needed to talk about our way forward. "Staff meeting at six tonight in the house."

Roland appeared nervous as he paced the kitchen. No one appeared to notice but me. After several seconds, he twisted his head and threw back his shoulders.

"Mickey," he said, his voice wavering, "would you like to have dinner with me tonight? I can pick you up after your meeting. Shall we say seven?" He stood back and waited for my response.

Everyone in the room was silent. All eyes were on me. Stunned by his invite, I looked from man to man. Killian and Keagan seemed to be amused, Kerrick appeared unhappy. I wondered why he would be upset. Wasn't that what he wanted—for me to move on?

Roland's eyes shone with anticipation. There was no way I was crushing his ego in front of three other men. "Yes, that sounds like fun. What did you have in mind?" I looked around and found the younger McKinleys staring at Kerrick. His face was unreadable, but there seemed to be a chill in the air. If I didn't know better, I'd have said he was jealous.

"I thought we'd go to Trevi's Steakhouse, but if you prefer somewhere else, I'm happy to take you anywhere." He appeared so pleased with himself.

"Steak sounds fabulous. I can't wait." The three brothers would have to fend for themselves. I had a date. "You're on your own for dinner, boys."

Clean up was quick. Roland and the younger McKinleys headed back to the stables, leaving Kerrick and me alone.

"Are you going to date the veterinarian?" He stood in front of me, blocking my way.

Putting my hand up to his cheek, I caressed the scruff I'd grown to love. "What do you care?" I didn't know if I should be flattered or angry. How many times had he rebuffed my advances? "I'm not dating him, we're having dinner. That's all."

"You're kidding, right? I'm a man. He's not looking for dinner. I watch him look at you. He wants more than dinner. He wants you." He said this with some distaste in his voice.

"Really? I've known him since we were kids. He's never been interested before."

"Don't be stupid. He's a man, and you're an easy target." His reference to my being easy ignited a fire in me. Hot with fury, I pushed past him and walked toward the stable. "What? I'm just telling you the facts."

"I may have been easy for you, but I've learned my lesson. I thought you were worth my time, but I was wrong. Remember, with us it was sex; with him it could be more. Don't worry, I'll take my time. I might wait a day or two before I strip naked and take him on the barn floor." Furious, I walked to the tack room to grab Mr. Darcy's saddle.

Slamming the door behind us, he pushed me against the wall,

pinning me to the hard wooden planks. His hardness dug into my hip as he pressed himself against me.

"This is what you do to me, Mickey. You have no idea what power you have. A glance in my direction, and I'm hard as a rock. A stroke of your hand across my arm can make me come." His lips crushed against mine in a bruising kiss. My hands grabbed a hold of his hair and held him in place while I took what he offered. His kisses made me want more. A moan escaped my lips as his hand traveled under my shirt to tweak my nipple. His knee spread my legs apart. I pushed my center against him and ground my sex into his leg. I wanted him so badly. I needed to feel him inside me again.

"God, Mickey, you drive me fucking out of my mind." His hand left my breast and slid down my stomach into the top of my jeans. My snug fitting pants left little room for maneuvering. Tugging at the button, I pulled them free. With the pull of a zipper, I was no longer trussed up in denim. All I could think about was him—inside me. Long fingers spread me apart and slipped inside my wetness. His mouth silenced my groans of pleasure. With his fingers deep inside me, I pressed against him, trying to soothe the deep ache within me.

"Kerrick, if you don't have sex with me, I'll lose my shit." My hips ground out a rhythm against his hand that promised to satisfy my desire. "I've needed you for days, and you've ignored me." A tingling sensation raced from my center and wormed its way up my back. Right before the sensation could connect with my brain, voices on the other side of the door interrupted everything and sent the feelings plummeting. Kerrick backed away as if I'd slapped him. The door handle turned. I fumbled with my pants, managing to right myself just before the door swung open. *Shit, SHIT.*

"This one, right?" Kerrick asked as he pulled the saddle off the rack.

"Yep," I said, breathless, as I took the bridle and pad from the wall. "Thanks for your help." I walked out of the room, ready to throttle anyone in my path. The others must have sensed my frustration. They cut a wide berth around me as I walked past them and out of the tack room. Kerrick walked the saddle out to the paddock and left me to saddle my horse.

Ten minutes later, we were mounted and riding toward open space. No one was saying a word. Left shaking and needy, riding Mr. Darcy soothed my frayed nerves. The miracle of his arrival couldn't be overlooked. The universe was smiling on me, if only by returning my horse. I took a deep breath and raised my eyes to the sky. Rolling my neck, I tried to reclaim equilibrium.

"Wait up." Kerrick pulled his horse beside me. "What are you so angry about?" He leaned over, grabbed the reins from me and pulled me to a stop. His riding skills were superior. Not only did he stop my progress, he did it in a way that didn't feel threatening to my horse.

"Everything. I'm angry at having to start my life over because some asshole of a man decided to screw me over. I'm angry I'm in a precarious financial situation. There are so many things I'm pissed at right now, but do you know what agitates me the most? I'm angry with myself for panting after you like a bitch in heat and having you toss me aside. You enter the room, and I fucking melt at the sight of you. My insides clench the minute you're near. What I'm really wondering is, is it you, or the fact that I've been celibate for two years?"

He sat atop his horse, stunned by my words. "Mickey—" he began but was stopped by my angry retort.

"Save it. I'm done begging for you to take me. I thought I wanted you, but maybe any man will do. I've got to go. I have a meeting and a date to prepare for. Enjoy your ride." His head slammed back as if I'd punched him. What was it I saw in his expression? Was it anger or hurt? Whatever it was, I didn't have time to spend on a man who had no capacity to give me anything but a hard time, both literally and figuratively. Turning my mount, I rode Mr. Darcy back to the stables.

The next hour was spent grooming him and settling him into his stall. Kerrick returned with Keen. He talked to his horse as if he were human. I admired that about him. He treated his animal like

Set Free

he would a lover, and that saddened me. Deep inside, I knew that he would be the kind of man who would love deeply.

He barely knew me, and he'd seen to my care and protection with the dedication of a secret service agent. He'd loaned me his family, taken care of Morgan, and satisfied my initial sexual needs. I wanted more, and he was unable or unwilling to give it—and that pissed me off.

Now there was Roland. Why did I say yes to him? He was a nice man, but he did nothing for me. If I was honest with myself, I did it to see if I could get a rise out of Kerrick. I almost got what I was looking for in the middle of the tack room. *Yes, there was certainly a rise there…*

In my attempt to look nice for my date, I applied makeup and put on a dress and heels. Thankfully, I had put some weight back on and my clothes were beginning to fit better. By five forty-five, I was ready for the McKinleys to arrive. On the table, I placed the six-pack of beer and a notepad. At six o'clock sharp, the three men walked into the house. I was surprised to see Kerrick but reminded myself that I had begged him to move back in with me until the entire Morgan debacle was over. It wasn't enough that I wanted him, but I had to insist he was close enough to torture my senses. *Glutton for punishment.*

Kerrick grabbed a beer and scanned me from tip to toe. What was his problem? He pushed me away, and then eye-fucked me every time he saw me. He walked to the couch and flipped on the television. Grateful he didn't plan to stay for the meeting, I discussed the needs of the ranch as it pertained to our new vision.

Several decisions were made concerning purchases and money-saving practices. Killian was in charge of saving us five dollars a bale by picking up the hay. That simple cost-saving strategy would cut the feeding costs by a third. With the exception of Keen, the ranch would charge seven hundred dollars a month for full boarding. This was a top-notch facility, and providing full care for a minimum of ten horses would keep the staff fed and housed throughout the winter.

The grazing fees would provide the income needed to purchase the necessary equipment for breeding and converting a portion of the barn into a breeding shed. A sixty/forty split was agreed upon for breeding fees. I insisted the McKinleys got the larger portion, since I'd be nowhere without their horses and expertise.

Headlights shone through the window just before seven. All eyes went from the window, to me, and then to Kerrick. His face was unreadable. I walked around the table to pick up my purse and reached the door just before Roland knocked.

Chapter 12

MICKEY

"You look wonderful, Mickey." His words were sweet. Sadly, I got a stronger reaction when Kerrick told me something about my too-skinny ass.

"Thanks. I wasn't sure what to wear. It's been a long time since I've been out to a nice dinner." I turned to wave goodbye and found myself staring into the eyes of an angry detective.

Confused by his ever-changing behavior, I shook my head and walked out the door.

Dinner was a pleasant affair. The food was excellent, and the company engaging. Roland was the sibling I'd never had. We talked about various topics, from family to animals, and ended our evening talking about the McKinleys.

"Do you and Kerrick have something going on? I thought he might pull his weapon and shoot me while we were leaving." I thought back to the fear-inducing look Kerrick gave us when we left the house.

"No. I thought we shared a connection, but he made it clear he wasn't interested in pursuing a relationship." I tried to pretend that it was nothing, but deep inside it tore me up to have shared such intimate moments with a man who didn't care.

"He's an idiot. Who wouldn't want a relationship with you? You're sweet and compassionate. You love animals. I'd love a relationship with you." He stared at me with something akin to a question in his eyes. Was he asking for permission to proceed?

"You're a great guy, Roland—"

"But…" he said and rolled his eyes.

"No buts. You're a great guy, and I've enjoyed dinner. It feels a bit like I'm with family, and I could use a family."

"Right, somehow that sounds so wrong." The face he made was a mirror of how I felt. Nose crinkled, mouth askew.

It broke my heart that he couldn't be the one. He was everything a woman could hope for. He was employed, cute, smart, and sweet. However, a relationship with him would feel like incest.

"There's no reason we can't go out as friends. I like your company. I like you, but not in a romantic way. I thought maybe we could venture in that direction, but you're just too familiar to me. I see you as that boy I grew up with, the brother I never had." He grabbed his chest as if I'd pierced his heart.

"You're killing me, Mickey. Are you punishing me for calling you names and teasing you about your skinny legs?"

I laughed. "Of course not. Kerrick seems to think my ass is too skinny, and I didn't hold it against him."

"That proves my point, he's a dolt. Your ass is perfect."

We spent the remainder of the night talking about the new mission of the ranch. He was excited to be a part of the team and couldn't wait for the breeding to begin. He would take on a big part of the artificial insemination component of the business. Extracting, storing, and shipping champion horse semen was a tricky endeavor.

He talked about how impressed he was with Keagan and Killian, and how lucky I was to have them on board. I thought about Kerrick and knew that without his help, I'd never be going in the direction I was.

We arrived back at the ranch just before eleven. Roland walked me to the door and leaned in to give me a kiss on the cheek. The door swung open right before his lips touched.

"I thought I heard a car pull up." Kerrick stood on the threshold and stared at us both.

"Is he living here?" Roland asked.

"Yes, for now, or until we find Morgan. Given Morgan's violent tendencies, we felt it better that he stay in the house. I'm hoping things fall into place soon, so everyone can get their life back on track."

"Oh, well, that seems reasonable." He dismissed Kerrick and said, "I got her for now. You can go back inside. I'll make sure she gets to bed just fine."

The two men stared at each other. Roland's dismissal of Kerrick was anything but brotherly. He made it sound as if he were going to personally take me to bed. Kerrick went back inside and slammed the door shut.

I grabbed Roland and pulled him away from the door. "You know he carries a gun, right?" We walked together toward the stables to check on the horses. Getting Roland away from my front door seemed to be the smartest choice.

"I'm pushing his buttons. It's what men do. He doesn't know that you're not interested in me. So, why not make him sweat a bit? Do you like him, Mickey?"

"Yes, more than I should, but he's not interested in me." That pebble of truth hurt.

"He's interested. You can tell by his eyes, and the way he tries to get larger when I'm around." He guided me in front of him as we entered the stables. "If he weren't interested in you, why would he almost take you in the tack room? Your heavy breathing was a dead giveaway." I was grateful I was walking ahead of him. The color of my cheeks must have been crimson.

"He may be interested in that, but he's not interested in anything else."

"Don't let his attempt at indifference fool you. It doesn't fool his brothers or me. I knew you liked him when I asked you out. A piece of me wished it to be otherwise."

I turned around with my hands on my hips. "You asked me out to irritate him?"

"Not exactly. I asked you out to see where his intentions lay. Did you see him when we left? He acted like a small child throwing a silent tantrum. He watched you like a hawk, Mickey, and it wasn't because he has some misplaced sense of obligation to protect you. He's not even assigned to you."

"I suppose, but I think it's just in his makeup to help. How do you know so much about him?"

"His brothers told me his story." We walked around, checking on the horses. "I guess you need to try to convince him he's ready to move on. He'll protect and look after you, and maybe you can protect and look after him." The sincerity in his face was humbling. He stood there, lobbying for another man, right after I'd turned him down. That took courage.

We walked back to the house. At the door, he bent down and kissed my cheek. I felt as though I'd gained a friend. Something I desperately needed.

Chapter 13

MICKEY

The next few weeks raced by in a blur. The conversion work on the barn was complete, and Keagan had begun the breeding practice. It was late in the season, so he used lights to stimulate the reproductive systems of the mares. The stallions were brought in to cover the mares several times a day. It was an aggressive act and required everyone to be on guard to make sure the horses didn't get injured.

Roland came in a few times a week to check on things and seemed quite pleased with the way operations were going. He had been instrumental in getting several of the stalls filled with boarders. The ranch had nine horses to care for, not including the six brought in with the McKinleys.

There had been no sign of Morgan in the last few weeks; it was like he'd dropped off the face of the Earth.

The lawyer delivered his eviction notice and a copy of the will written in laymen's terms. Both documents had been sealed and posted to Morgan's door in case he showed up unnoticed.

Kerrick had finished moving his things into the cabin, but he still spent his time in my house. We had settled into a routine. He skulked around, looking miserable, while I longed for him to break free of his self-imposed ban on relationships. I plugged through my days, wishing our situation were different.

Roland had taken me out three times. Each time, he made sure Kerrick was around to see us leave. It was funny to watch him feign indifference when the tightness of his jaw was a dead giveaway to his distress. It would be so easy to pull him aside and take anything he offered, but my days of impulsivity were waning. It was time to take control of my life and emotions.

The nights were the hardest, knowing that he was in the room next to mine was almost unbearable. Walking into the kitchen to find him just showered and nude above the waist was torture. Did he do that on purpose? Something told me he did.

Today was no different from the rest. I rose early to care for the horses and found him sitting in front of his computer at the kitchen table. Water droplets ran down his chest as he sat in nothing but a towel. It sat open at his leg and showed his thigh all the way to the crease below his hip. My eyes scanned his body. I thought about how it would feel to run my tongue up his leg. To lick the drop of water that was now running down his nipple. I wet my lip with my tongue. Looking at him made my throat dry and my lady parts wet. His cough pulled me from my happy place.

"Do you like what you see?" His question was laced with seduction. The warm tone of his voice washed over me like sensual oil. Why did he play this game with me? I was a yo-yo attached to his string.

"What?" Ripped out of my inappropriate thoughts, I tried to process his words.

"I was just wondering if you liked what you saw. You were devouring me whole." Looking down at his tented towel, he grinned. "Your hungry look seems to have elicited a response from me."

"Well, that's a shock. Usually, the only response I get from you is agitation and indifference." I walked past him and into the kitchen to pour coffee. Looking at his straining erection hobbled me. It was disgusting how much control he had over me simply because he owned a dick. Had my life come down to that? When did that happen? Oh yeah, that first day he took me to bed and showed me the wonders of his manhood.

After pouring coffee, I walked back into the dining room.

"What are you so pissed about? I'm just teasing you." He stood up and almost dropped the towel.

With agitation taking over, I shook with frustration. "That's the problem, you're a tease. You pull me in with seductive innuendo, and the minute I respond, you retreat. They call girls who do that a cock-tease, but what do they call men?" I paused for a minute and then continued. "Oh, that's right, they call them cowards." I turned to leave, but he moved to block my exit before he laid into me.

"What's your problem? You're dating the veterinarian, and you're angry because I won't put out? Have you lost your fucking mind? You fawn all over that man each time he comes to the ranch, which is too often. You spend hours on end watching horses mate, and then disappear into the office to do who knows what."

"What? I spend time with Roland because he's taking care of the horses. He's also making arrangements for the storage and shipping of specimens to our buyers." He was jealous of Roland. "We spend time in the office preparing documents on pedigrees and procedures. We are not dating, and we're not doing what your dirty mind thinks we're doing. He's like a brother to me. If I didn't know better, I'd think you were jealous, but that couldn't be, because you would have to invest something to feel that way, and you're an empty account—emotionally bankrupt." I walked toward the office and slammed the door.

Several minutes later, the door opened slowly. Behind it peeked a sullen man, still dressed in a towel. *God, he was going to be the death of me.*

"Can we talk?" He walked in and sat in front of my desk. How was I supposed to talk to him when all I wanted to do was have him bend me over the desk and pound into me?

"You talk, and I'll listen." I didn't have much more to say on the matter. I wanted him, and he wasn't available.

"I like you, Mickey, more than I'd like to. I want you in ways you can't even imagine." He had no idea how active my imagination could be. "It's not that I don't have emotions. I'm afraid." The pain in his face caused my empathy gene to fire up. Gone was sarcasm, arrived was concern. I could observe what he felt in the sadness of his eyes and the slump of his posture.

"Why?" I didn't want to press, but he was confusing me again. His normal game of push and pull.

"I told you when we first met that it was sex, and that was it. After the first time, I knew it would always be more with you. That's why I walked away. The second time was pure weakness on my part."

"I don't understand. You told me you weren't relationship material. You've done everything in your power to make me believe you had no interest in me, and now you're telling me you knew right away that it would always be something more with me? You're an asshole."

"That's my point, I'm an asshole. I'm not good for you." He leaned across the table and tried to take my hands, but I pulled them out of his reach.

"How convenient for you to use that excuse. I'm twenty-four years old, and I've known some assholes in my time. Morgan was the biggest. He took advantage of me in ways that you never could. Maybe you aren't good for me, but shouldn't that be my decision? You'll never know, because you're paralyzed by your own fear. If you were a good detective, you would have figured out that I'm not a girl who gives up easily. Hell, I stayed with a man who beat me because I thought it was what my father would have wanted. Has it ever occurred to you that I might be good for you?" Pushing back from my desk, I rose and walked out of the room.

Irritated with his shortsighted attitude, I took my frustrations out in the stables. I cleaned the stalls in record time. By mid-morning, I walked into the barn to find Keagan standing by Brody. Killian was calming the mare in the breeding shoot, while Kerrick watched the scene unfold. His eyes caught and held mine for a moment. The rearing of the mare grabbed everyone's attention.

Not all the mares were up for getting mounted on demand, and this one was fighting the process. Kerrick stepped in to help by pulling her to the front of the pen. Brody, being the stud he was, made quick work of his job. He seemed to know what was expected and liked getting it done quickly so he could get back to his oats.

Within minutes, both horses were removed from the pen and taken back to their stalls. Throughout the whole process, Kerrick's eyes never left me. His look was feral.

"Mickey?" I knew he had more to say, but I wasn't sure I was willing to listen. Without waiting for an answer or confirmation, he placed his hand on the small of my back and escorted me to the house. Pulling out the chair, he sat me at the table.

"What?" I didn't mean to sound so abrasive, but there was nothing else to say.

"I've been thinking about what you said this morning. You're right. I'm paralyzed, but not from the fear of starting something. I'm paralyzed from the fear of you ending what we begin."

"What?" This time my words were soft and seeking. He was exposing his vulnerable self, and I was transfixed.

"At first, I came up with the rationale that you were bad for me because I was in law enforcement and you were a criminal. That lasted as far as our first kiss. Then I convinced myself that it would be pure sex, but our connection was too strong. My last thread of hope was that you were with Roland. This morning you tell me he's like a brother. I'm finished trying to avoid you. I don't want to anymore. I was trying to protect myself, and in the process, I still hurt you."

Sitting in stunned silence, I had no idea how to respond. "What are you telling me? Is this a game with you? You open your heart and I fall in, and then tomorrow you get scared and close me out again? I can't ride this roller coaster with you. I've got serious stuff to take care of around here. I've got one crazy man in my life, I don't have room for another. You're either in or out, but you can't be both." My heart pounded in my chest as I gave him an ultimatum. Would he step up and try to be the man I wanted and needed, or would he continue to hide behind his broken heart?

"I'm in. I want to do it right. I want to take you to dinner and dancing. I want to hold your hand in front of that twatwad cashier and know that when I call you honey, it's authentic. I want to kiss you in front of the world and let every ogling man know you're off limits, especially Roland. You may think of him like a brother, but I see him look at you, and I don't like it. If he's a brother, then he's an incestuous little bastard." He pulled me from the chair and wrapped me in his arms. The feel of his body against mine was bliss, but I remained cautious.

"What now, Detective?"

"Watching Brody mount that mare has given me some thoughts. I'm tired of him being the only one on this ranch with a sex life." He lifted me and carried me toward my room.

"Is this going to turn into an only-about-the-sex moment?" If he tried to run after today, I might be going back to prison after I killed him.

"Nope, this is something different—something more."

"Stop talking and take me to bed. I'm tired of waiting for you." He passed through the door and tossed me on the bed. I struggled with the button to my jeans as I frantically tried to get my pants off.

"Hey, stop." *Oh hell no, he wasn't going to change his mind again, was he?* "Mickey, there's no rush. It's gonna be an afternoon in bed. We're making love this time, not having sex."

His words stilled my beating heart. He wanted to make love. That required a level of commitment. He wanted to spend the afternoon in bed. That required his full attention.

Lying on my back, I breathed out the tension in my taught body and relaxed. With my arms spread open, I waited for him to make the next move.

Planting kisses across my face, his lips landed on mine in a gentle but passionate kiss. I opened my mouth to his and let his probing tongue fill me with heat. It was funny how a kiss could cause so much friction between my legs. Button by button, he unfastened my shirt and spread it open to reveal my lace bra. Searing lips scorched my breasts through the fabric. I squirmed. I panted. I begged.

"Please, you're killing me. I've wanted you for weeks, and you held me at arm's length. Now you're in my bed, and you're still keeping your distance. I. Want. You. In. Me." I screamed the words at him. Pulling at his shirt, I managed to unfasten the top two buttons and get my hand inside to feel the coarse hair on his chest.

Removing my hands from his shirt, he placed them above my head and secured them with one hand. "Do I need to go to my truck and get my cuffs? I'm not beyond tying you up to slow you down." It took a minute for me to comprehend what he was saying.

"You wouldn't."

"I would. In fact, I kind of like the idea of you cuffed and at my mercy. I feel like I've been at yours for weeks. Turnabout is fair play."

"That's not fair. I didn't do anything to you. You put yourself in emotional handcuffs, and I had nothing to do with it." He pulled at the button on my jeans, setting it free.

"You had everything to do with it. You're a walking seductress, and you have no idea you're doing it."

His fingers tugged at the zipper. He was inches away from where I needed his touch to be. Breathless, I begged for him again.

"Patience. We have all afternoon." He pulled my jeans side to side. Once they cleared my hips, I kicked them down to my ankles. With my pants stuck at my boots, I was trapped. My arms were in his grip, and my legs were held hostage by my bunched-up pants.

"Please," I begged. "Remember, I'm a multiples girl. You can make me come several times, and I won't complain." His laughter silenced me.

"I imagine you wouldn't complain. I'd hope not anyhow. I'm letting go of your hands, but you need to leave them above your head. I'm going to take off your boots and pants. Understand?"

Nodding my head, I left my hands exactly where they were. Ripples of desire rushed through me. The cool air hit my heated flesh just before his mouth.

I didn't dare move my hands, even though I wanted to thread my fingers through his hair and hold him between my legs. Fear that he might stop glued them in place. My hips bucked until he used his hands to hold them down.

"Slow down, Sugar. It's been a long time since I feasted on you, and I plan to take my time." His lips rolled over my flesh, their heat burning into me. His tongue stroked me in a languid, unhurried fashion.

Trying to calm my breathing, I focused on the sensations. Gentle and wet, he lapped at me, pulling and nipping at my skin. He dipped his tongue into my heat, then retreated to start all over again. He was like a hungry man at a banquet. With trembling knees, I lifted up and pressed against his lips. Rising. Reaching. Seeking my release.

He crawled up my body and continued his feast on my breasts. A tug of my lace bra released them into his hands. His calloused fingers rubbed the pebbled tips, sending shivers of delight straight between my legs.

"I love these," he said as he cupped them. I lifted my head and watched his tongue lick at my erect nipple. To watch this man honor my body undid me. I lay naked under his fully clothed form.

"I'm naked, and you're not," I said in a ragged voice. "Take your clothes off." I pulled my stiff arms from above my head and helped him unbutton his shirt the rest of the way. He made quick work of his remaining clothes and scooted in close to my body, his skin against mine, my body wrapped around his.

It was my time to explore. With my legs straddling his body, I trailed my kisses down his face to his neck. Slick lips and a moist tongue made quick work of exploring his chest. I gained great confidence by the hitching of his breath and the pitching of his hips. He was not immune to my ministrations either. My hands explored every inch of him as I slid down his body. His hardness bobbed in front of my eager lips, and I took him into my mouth.

"Oh my God, you're going to kill me. What do you call that move?"

"I'm just tastin' your peach, Sugar." I gave him my best southern twang.

"I knew you were bad news the minute I picked you up." His hands threaded through my hair and guided me into a steady rhythm of his choosing. The smoothness of his skin felt like silk against my tongue. I rocked my body on the bed trying to find my release. At this point, anything could put me over the edge. "Stop. I don't want to be done so soon."

It pained me to stop.

He flipped me onto my back and continued where he left off. His tongue, lips, and fingers were everywhere. My skin prickled with something electrifying. Every touch jolted me into awareness. His fingers eased into me and filled the emptiness inside. His thumb massaged my tiny bundle of nerves with steady pressure. He slid in, then out. My muscles clenched around him. My body vibrated. It was almost too much to handle. Almost.

Shaking with need, I whimpered and begged for him to let me fly. In and out, his deliberate strokes built toward the ultimate release. It was coming. Tingling, burning pleasure, heavy breathing and then…I screamed my release while my body pulsed around his probing fingers.

His lips wrapped around my nipple to draw out every quiver. I rolled away from the intensity of his touch. It was too much. Tears rolled down my face as a feeling of complete satisfaction washed over me.

His arms curled around my waist and pulled me into his side. I felt his hardness pulse against my backside. His hands caressed my arms while his lips pressed against my hair. I needed a minute to breathe.

"You're beautiful, Mickey. I'm sorry I was an ass. You're dangerous for me—dangerous for my heart. It was the peaches. I was sunk."

I rolled over and pressed my lips against his bare chest. His body was damp with perspiration.

"Peaches?" I teased. "What's this about peaches?" Reaching down, I held his thickness in the palm of my hand. He was heavy with desire. My touch sent a noticeable shiver up his body.

Groaning his pleasure, he took a deep breath and said, "Oh, something about smelling and sweetness and tasting. I wanted to taste you since that very first day. You planted the seed in my head, and I could never get it out. You taste like sweet nectar. It's why I call you Sugar. I'm addicted to you, to your taste."

"Make love to me. I've been waiting for weeks for you to want me." I rubbed suggestively against his body.

"I've wanted you the entire time." He closed my fingers around his erection. "Can't you feel how much I want you now? Let me get a condom." He tried to pull away from me to reach for his pants.

"We're good if you're okay without using one. I went and got the shot a few weeks ago. I was hoping we could enjoy each other without anything coming between us, and then you seemed like you didn't want me."

"Oh God, I'm so fucked."

I had always heard that the feeling was more intense without a condom. One of the ranch hands once described sex with a condom like licking a sucker still in its wrapper. It was still a sucker, he said, but it had no flavor.

"You sound like making love to me might be the worst possible thing." Was he that worried about losing his heart? Shit, after that orgasm, I'd never be able to be with anyone but him.

"No, it will be the best possible thing. The worst possible thing would be never getting to experience you. I was stupid, and now we've wasted weeks." He rose up and positioned himself over me. He didn't begin by pressing into me. He coaxed my body into a heightened state. Sensual kisses jolted my awareness, a twirl of his tongue across my hardened nipple sent my pulse racing. I could feel the dampness building between my legs. Reaching between them, he dragged his fingers across my skin. "You are so ready for me." Nudging against my entrance, he pushed and retreated. It was slow torture when all I wanted was to be completely filled by him. I pushed my hips up to meet his, but he pulled away. There was no hurry, he was taking his time. Inch by glorious inch, I stretched to receive him. He stroked me slowly with reverence. Never once did he take his eyes off me.

"Look at me," he demanded. "I want to see the passion in your eyes. I want to look into your soul and know that I've touched it deeply."

His words alone had tattooed me forever. What man told you

that he wanted to touch your soul? He wanted to strip me of everything, so in the end it was just the two of us; no one else mattered.

I stared into his eyes and felt his body rock against me. His movements demanded my response. He shifted his hips so that his hardness rubbed against my throbbing center. He pushed me to the edge and told me it was okay to jump. In my heart, I knew he would catch me.

The explosion in my body not only erupted in my core, but my heart, too. I trembled and shuddered with waves of pleasure washing over me. Never once did I take my eyes off the man above me. Something profound had occurred. It was like a melding of two bodies into one. I should be scared to death, but all I felt was unadulterated joy.

I knew when he found his release. His body stiffened, then shuddered. His mouth turned lax, and the look of bliss flowed over him. He collapsed half on and half off me. Everything about today was perfect.

Chapter 14

MICKEY

I woke up in the dark room and flew from the bed. How much time had passed? And where the hell was Kerrick? If he loved and left me, I'd never mend. He wasn't the only one recovering. I might not have a broken heart, but I was broken nonetheless. I distrusted men, and leaving me after making love to me wasn't going to help build trust.

I barely got my shirt pulled over my head when I heard him enter.

"Hey, what's wrong?" He walked over to me and pulled me into his arms.

The tears ran down my face. "I thought you left me. I thought maybe you decided it was just sex again and walked away. I woke up, and you were gone." His fingers gently wiped the tears from my face.

"I went to make you dinner. I thought you would be hungry after this afternoon. I threw a chicken in the oven. It will be finished in about forty-five minutes. I told the boys to be here at six-thirty. I didn't leave you. I'm not leaving you."

He crushed me against his chest and held me tight. I released the pent-up anxiety in the remaining tears I shed.

"I'm sorry. I'm programmed to expect disappointment. Did you say it was after five?" I laid my head against his chest and breathed in his scent. It was uniquely him and pure male.

"Yes, but don't worry, my brothers tended to the horses and everything is fine. Come here." He pulled me to the bed. I crawled into it wearing only a cotton shirt. He was dressed in only jeans. "Since we both have had miserable past experiences, let's establish some ground rules."

I stared at him for a moment. What did he mean by ground rules? "What are you talking about?"

"I'm talking about deal breakers. For example, cheating for me is a deal breaker. If we are together, then it's just you and me. No other men. Okay?" Given his history, I could understand why cheating would be at the top of his no-go list.

"I would never cheat," I told him. He leaned over my prone body and played with my hair. "No hitting. I never want to be hit by a man again. Even in play."

"Deal. I'm sorry I swatted your fabulous ass the first time." He gave me a wink.

"Oh, now it's fabulous? I thought I had a skinny ass."

"You did until I saw it up close and in person. Your baggy pants didn't do it justice. The few pounds you've put on are perfect."

"No lying, even if you think it's for my own good. I need to hear the truth about everything."

"I require the same from you." He leaned down to brush a kiss on my lips.

"What are we calling this thing between us? Do you want to keep it secret, or are we a couple?" Would he admit to having a relationship? That would be a big step for him.

"Mickey, I just poured my inner spirit into you. I've emptied myself completely, and you have to ask? You're mine. I'll tattoo it on your forehead, if that's what it requires."

"I've wanted to be yours since that first day in the grocery store, when you told me you didn't like a shaved pussy." His candor had always been attractive.

"Why did that make an impression?" He tilted his head in question.

"You didn't know me, and still you were honest. Not only that, but you stepped in to help a stranger, and you stayed even when things were grim." My hands roamed over his torso. His muscles felt thick and strong under my fingers.

"Will my job come between us? I get called at crazy hours. Crime isn't scheduled between nine and five." I saw his heartbeat accelerate, and his breathing become labored.

"Kerrick, I'm not your ex. You went back to work a week ago, and you always manage to make time for your brothers, your horse, and for me. I'm here all the time, so if you're here, then we have time whenever."

"You realize that you may never get rid of me, right? I'm not leaving your bed or your side." He didn't allow me to answer; his mouth covered mine, and all conversation halted. We emerged from the bedroom twenty minutes later, smiling.

Keagan and Killian filed into the house fifteen minutes following. If their goofy looks were any indication, they knew exactly what had been going on before their arrival. This was worse than getting caught in the barn kissing a ranch hand.

"How was your nap?" Keagan asked. Killian and he shared a glance, and both men laughed.

"All right, that's enough. Mickey will stop feeding you if you embarrass her. I'll kick your ass if you don't quit your teasing. Let's get it out in the open. Mickey and I are dating. She belongs to me, and I belong to her. I expect you two to continue to look after her as if she belonged to you, too." There were looks of surprise on his brothers' faces, while Kerrick grimaced at his poor choice of words. "Not that way, assholes. She will never belong to either of you that way."

With that out of the way, we sat down at the table and enjoyed the meal that Kerrick made for us. My Kerrick, the man who publicly claimed me. I felt like part of a family for the first time in a long time. Things were looking up.

Set Free

THE REST of the week flew by. The days were spent working on the ranch, and nights were spent making love.

The deal with Tom Morrow had worked out well. His use of the pastures had brought needed income to the ranch. The boys' breeding fees had brought the money needed to upgrade the barn. Everything seemed to be falling into place. The only problem was the whereabouts of Morgan. Kerrick had run several checks and hadn't been able to locate him.

The last time his bank account was used was to withdraw a substantial amount of cash, it was enough money to let him disappear for months.

"I'm heading to the store to buy groceries. Do you want to come?" I glided by Kerrick and placed my arms around his neck, planting a kiss on his cheek. He had been sitting in front of his computer all morning. He was working on closing out a case and had been writing up his report.

Grabbing me, he pulled me into his lap and nibbled on my chin. "I don't need food. I can live on you for the rest of my life." He better be careful, or I might take him up on it, and the whole ranch would wither away to nothing. And, I couldn't deny being eaten by Kerrick was a very pleasurable experience.

"That sounds promising, but how will you feel when your brothers are starving to death? Feeding them was part of the deal." I bit his lower lip and listened to him moan.

"I don't give a shit about them. How am I supposed to think about them when I have a hard-on and you on my lap?" I wiggled against the bulge in his pants. Yep, it was hard.

"Tell you what. You know that thing I do with my tongue when I taste your peach?" His brows shot up to his hairline. "I promise to do that and more later if you go to the store with me. I hate facing that bitch on my own." That seemed to get his attention. He almost dropped me to the floor when he rose from the chair.

"Let's go. I'm ready to shop." It was funny how the mention of single fruit could motivate that man. He grabbed my purse and rushed me out the door.

We grabbed enough food to get through the week. Kerrick pushed the cart to the front. I guided him away from the cashier I didn't like, but he pushed forward into her line.

As I unloaded the cart, Kerrick stood at the register. I knew he was up to something. "What's your name?" he asked the blonde. She seemed giddy from his question. Like asking her anything was an invitation to flirt. Yes, he was that gorgeous.

"I'm Lisa. What's your name, handsome?" She flipped her straw-like hair over her shoulder. The shit was deep.

"Detective McKinley." He flashed his badge in her face and shoved it back into his pocket. "Have you seen Morgan Canter since the night I threw you out of the cabin?" He said this loud enough for anyone within twenty feet to hear. By the look on her face, she appeared to understand that this was more of an interrogation than a social call.

"I've seen him around. He comes around my place every once in a while. He has that court date next week with her." She pointed at me and snarled the words.

"You need to tell him that his stuff is being donated to charity if he doesn't remove it from the premises immediately. His eviction notice has been posted for weeks. As his landlord, Mickey has no responsibility to store his personal belongings."

She replied without missing a beat. "That won't make him happy. He owns part of that ranch." The bitch was stupid enough to challenge my man.

"Actually, he doesn't. My girlfriend owns the ranch in its entirety. He was a hired hand that received equity *while* it was a cattle ranch. He sold the entire herd of cattle, therefore making his share zero. You'll give him the message, right, Lisa?" His tone was clear and condescending. There was a calm hardness that would brook no argument.

I stared openmouthed at Kerrick. He was deadly when he was on a mission. I pressed my lips to his and blurted out, "God, I love you. You are so sexy when you're in detective mode."

The cashier stood stunned in front of us. Kerrick took me into a passionate embrace and told me, "I love you, too. You're everything to me."

We leaned into each other and waited for the woman to give us a total.

"That's $373.12."

Kerrick handed her his credit card and said, "Thanks, Lisa. Don't forget, okay?" We packed up our bags and headed out the door.

Once in the car, Kerrick turned to me. "Was that you trying to get a reaction out of the cashier, or did you tell me you loved me?"

I leaned across the seat and pressed my body into his. I wanted him to feel what my heart already knew. My lips pressed into his. This wasn't a passionate kiss—it was a message. My hand rested on his chest. I felt it tighten as my love flowed through him. Words were just words; this was more. Much more.

"Any questions?" I asked while I buckled myself into the safety belt.

"Nope, I'm good." While we drove toward our home, I thanked the universe for him. When everything was going to hell, I was blessed with the luck of the Irish.

"Do you think he'll show up?" Morgan coming back to the ranch frightened me. "I'm scared that he might." My adrenaline pumped at the thought of seeing Morgan again. What would he do to me next?

"Yes, I think he'll come. He won't like hearing that he's a hired hand when he had such a different idea of his importance. I'm pretty sure she sees him more than she would like to admit. Did you see the shiner under her eye? She did a pretty good job of covering it, but it was still there."

I didn't notice the bruise. My attention was focused on him. It saddened me that the woman was willing to take Morgan's abuse, and then I reminded myself that I was that woman over a year ago, but I'd never be again. He might come to the ranch, but I'd be ready for him.

"Don't worry, Mickey. Between me and my brothers, he won't get near you."

I was worried, but I'd be ready. I never realized until now how my friends from prison inadvertently prepared me for him. Robyn taught me self-defense, and Megan offered her good sense and think-it-through instruction. Natalie taught me to see the humor in serious situations, and Holly showed me what loyalty was all about with her dedication to her mother. Hell, the woman did time because she refused to let her mother suffer. I didn't miss prison, but I missed my friends.

THE NEXT FEW days passed by uneventfully. I took the time to write the girls from Cell Block C. Holly was getting out of prison in under a month. I planned to be there waiting. We passed the days in normal fashion, only everyone seemed a bit edgier.

It was the end of the season, and Keagan and Killian spent their days in the barn with Brody and Diesel. When Kerrick was gone, I had to spend my time there as well. I wished I could have spent that time with Mr. Darcy. I would've rather been crooning to him than standing by and watching horses mate all day.

When Kerrick left for work Wednesday, he pulled me into a bear hug and told me to be careful. He escorted me to his brothers before he drove off the property.

Two more boarders had been added, raising the number of paid guests to eleven. The ranch was busy, and it felt good to know we were creating something wonderful together.

Tired of watching the boys mate Brody to every available mare, I snuck out of the barn and headed to the stables. It had been a few days since I'd ridden Mr. Darcy. When I reached his stall, I noticed that he wasn't himself. He was lying on his side. His breathing was labored, and there was a discharge coming from his nose. I lay down next to him and pressed my ear to his chest. He whinnied and tried to right himself, but he didn't seem to have the energy.

My back pocket held my phone. I needed Roland now. Empty. I

must have left it on the table when I kissed Kerrick goodbye. My horse needed help. "I'll be right back. I have to get my phone." With my eyes on Mr. Darcy, I dashed out of the stable but came to a dead stop when I ran into a solid wall of muscle. Feeling relieved that one of the men had come to check on me, I began to ramble.

"Call Dr. Mallory, I need him. Mr. Darcy is sick." I expected to find Keagan or Killian, but instead I was looking into the eyes of Morgan. He gave me a full body once-over, his eyes gleaming with dark intent. I struggled to keep the world from crashing in on top of me. *Breathe, damn it.*

Backing away, I told him, "You aren't allowed to be within one hundred yards of me." He stalked me step for step. I continued to back away. He pressed me deeper into the stables.

"Who's going to stop me? The men are in the barn. They won't hear a thing. You've seen that stud breed. He makes his mares squeal with delight. Noisy motherfuckers. I'm going to make you squeal, Mickey. It's been a long time, and you fucking owe me." Unkempt, his hair hung limply to the side. His clothes were tattered and soiled. How did I ever find this man attractive?

"I don't owe you anything. You've already taken more than your share. Where is the money for the cattle, Morgan? You nearly bankrupted the ranch." If I could keep him talking, maybe I could come up with a plan. My eyes scanned the perimeter of the stalls looking for a weapon. Without one, I was in trouble. He was double my weight and a foot taller than me.

"Shut the fuck up, Mickey. I'm so tired of you." He hovered over me like a massive dark cloud.

"Morgan, let me call the vet for Mr. Darcy, he's sick. He's sick, and he needs help." I pleaded with him to help my horse.

"It's too late for Darcy, Mickey. He has quite the appetite for oleander. It will be an agonizing death for him, but it should be quick. Too bad he had to suffer because of you. Did you think you could take something from me without paying a price yourself?" He stepped forward.

"Morgan stop." I stepped back. Running out of room to run, I panicked.

"How in the hell did you get him back? I had planned to come in and poison one of your boarders, but you made it so much more exciting when I found him. Imagine my surprise to find your beloved horse back in the stables."

Tears spilled down my face. How could he kill my horse? What did I ever do to earn the wrath of Morgan Canter? "Why, Morgan? What is this about?" I backed up again. I needed to get some help. If I yelled, he'd be on me in a second. He was fast for a big man. I was on my own.

"I understood the terms of the will. I was golden while we were together, but you were pulling away. I was pissed at you. I knew it was just a matter of time before you asked me to leave. You might have been uneducated about the will, but you've never been stupid. You would have figured it out eventually." He gave me a look that could boil the skin off a body. "Lisa was a distraction. I didn't expect you to react the way you did. Who would have thought you would be jealous?"

"I wasn't jealous, you stupid, egotistical pig. You tried to rape me. When I fought back, you beat me. I'm surprised I had the strength to puncture your tires or swing the iron. I had a broken rib and a bruised spleen. The police were supposed to arrest you, not me."

"It worked out beautifully. I couldn't have orchestrated it better myself. I got my share of the ranch anyway."

I had backed myself into a corner. He was looming over me, his breath hot and rancid. My only hope was to surprise him. With as much force as I could muster, I kneed him between the legs. With a groan, he doubled over and I got a second's head start. Sadly, it wasn't enough to get away. I almost made it to the entry when his hand circled my ankle, sending me crashing to the ground. I screamed at the top of my lungs. Morgan was right. There was no one to hear me. My screams would go unanswered. I anxiously searched for something—anything to slow him down.

"Morgan, please. Leave me alone." I begged for his mercy. I sent a prayer to the heavens asking for help, anything to get this man out of my life for good.

"Oh, now you're begging me. I dreamed of you begging me, but it didn't play out like this. In my dream, you were naked." I spider walked myself away from him, but he straddled my hips, pinning me under him. His big hand grabbed a hold of my shirt, stripping the buttons and leaving me exposed. "Now we're talking." He stared at my bare flesh and reached for my breast, but I swatted him away.

"I belong to Kerrick. Don't touch me." The feel of his sweaty palm against my face was a shock. It wasn't a surprise, but the force was startling. Feeling wetness on my lips, I pulled my hand away and saw the blood he'd drawn. Enraged, I turned on him like a caged animal, beating against his chest with the force of a jackhammer. He wasn't used to me fighting back.

His surprise gave me enough time to grab whatever I could to defend myself. Reaching out, I gripped the shovel, the one I was always telling Kerrick to put back. I could kiss that man if he were here. The shovel he had put back might save my life.

Winding up with full force, I swung blindly and waited for the impact. Pain shot through my hands as soon as I connected. The sound was sickening. A crackling of bones, a scream, and a thump, then nothing.

I raced from the stables to the barn with my tattered shirt hanging from my body and my lip dripping blood. Killian was the first to reach me.

"Oh my God, Mickey. What the hell happened?"

"Morgan. Call Roland now. Call Kerrick." I collapsed into a heap of tears.

The McKinleys jumped into action. Killian removed his shirt and covered my exposed chest. Keagan took off to the stables. Somewhere in the commotion, I heard Killian calling Roland. He told the vet he didn't know what the problem was, but I needed him.

"Mr. Darcy," I whispered.

Killian turned white as he talked to Kerrick. The roar coming from the phone would send anyone running in fear. I fought to free myself from Killian's grip. My horse needed me. Stumbling out of the barn, I made my way back to the stables. Keagan stood over an unconscious Morgan, guarding him in case he woke up and bolted.

I ran to Mr. Darcy and fell next to him. I whispered in his ear, I wanted to soothe his pain, soften his passing. I shifted myself to place his head in my lap. If his breathing was any indication, he didn't have much time. *Hang on, Mr. Darcy. You just got home, it's not time to leave me yet.* My tears fell onto his chestnut coat. My hand ran the length of his neck. Then nothing. He was gone.

Gone.
No breath.
Burning tears.
Gone.
Heartbreaking.
Darkness.
Gone.
Dead.

Flashing lights lit up the night sky. What time was it? The sun had set, the air was cool. I raised my head and saw several people running about. I was numb. Kerrick stood off to the side, looking toward me. His hard look sent shivers down my spine. What had I done? Oh God, had I killed Morgan?

I searched for him in the crowd of people. The only people I recognized were Killian, Keagan, and Roland. Their faces were sullen, defeated. The officer talking to Kerrick seemed familiar, and then it dawned on me: he was my arresting officer. He was back to do it again.

Resigned to my fate, I sat on my front porch and waited for the cuffs. I hadn't expected to see my friends for months, but it looked like we'd have an early reunion.

The officer approached me. I knew the drill. I pulled my hands behind my back and turned around.

"Ms. Mercer, I know it's been a difficult night for you, but would you be willing to give me your statement?"

The softness and compassion in his voice stunned me. I turned around and stumbled back to the bench.

"Huh?"

"I want to make sure that Mr. Canter doesn't get an opportunity to slip through the cracks. In order to do that, I need your statement." He placed his hand on my forearm in a caring gesture.

Kerrick looked at me with a pained expression. "Give him your statement sweetheart." He leaned in, brushed the lightest kiss against my tender lips and whispered, "I'm so sorry," before he turned and walked away.

"What happened here?" The officer's tone was low-key and comforting. He coaxed the information out of me. *No, I wasn't raped.* I heard an audible exhale from Kerrick, who was standing nearby. He'd been holding his breath, and now he seemed able to breathe. *Yes, Morgan assaulted me. Yes, he killed my horse.* The questions were asked several different ways. It always ended with my smashing him on the side of the head with a shovel. He was alive and guaranteed to live. I wasn't sure how I felt about that. On some level, he deserved to die for killing Mr. Darcy. On the other hand, he deserved to be incarcerated for his crimes.

Finally, the police left…without me. Kerrick paced. His body rigid, his face full of emotion—pain? Back and forth he traversed the porch. I shivered in the evening breeze, but it was his coolness that settled in my body. He lifted me and carried me into the house. Once he set me on the couch, he placed hot cocoa in my hands and disappeared into the bathroom. I swore I heard the sound of water, but everything was a blur.

He lifted me from the couch and walked me into the bathroom. Gentle hands removed my clothes. I relaxed for the first time in hours. Hot bubbly water pulled the strain from my muscles. The tears continued to flow. Was it really over?

The thud of the shovel against his head wouldn't stop replaying in my mind. The whinnying of Mr. Darcy just before his final breath hollowed me out.

Kerrick helped me from the tub and got me ready for bed. We lay together, him wrapped around my body. He hadn't said much. His silence said it all. The last thing I remembered before I slept was Kerrick telling me he was sorry he had failed me.

I woke up feeling like I'd been hit by a tractor-trailer. Every muscle was sore. My lip throbbed. My head ached. I felt around the bed for Kerrick, but his side was empty.

I dragged my weary body from the bed and visited the bathroom. Thankfully, I didn't look as bad as I felt.

After a quick shower, I tossed on my clothes and headed into the empty kitchen—no coffee—no Kerrick. Maybe he'd slept in the room next door.

I opened the door and found the space empty, not a trace of his existence to be found. My mind raced to remember everything from the night before. My stomach lurched as I recalled his goodnight message. "I'm sorry I failed you." How could he do that to me? At my lowest moment, he'd abandoned me?

Angry, I marched to the stables. My heart sank as I walked by Mr. Darcy's stall. He'd already been taken away. Roland would have seen to him right away, and I hoped that he'd disposed of his remains in a gentle and humane way.

Blurry eyes hindered my ability to see, but it was apparent the horses had been cared for that morning. Voices floated in from the paddock. I went in search of the source. Walking back from the field were four men: Killian, Keagan, Roland, and Kerrick. My heart swelled with hope when I saw him. He hadn't left me after all. Running toward them, I threw myself into Kerrick.

"Good morning. Did you get any sleep?" He eyed me with caution. He gave me a squeeze and set me aside. It was not the kind of greeting I'd hoped to receive. My heart was breaking, and I needed to be in the arms of the man I loved. I nodded my head and scanned the somber faces of the other men present.

"We buried your horse just outside of the cemetery. I hope that's okay." Concern was written all over Roland's face. The mention of Mr. Darcy released the floodgates once more. All four men seemed uncomfortable in the midst of my tears. Kerrick's brothers and Roland made up some excuse to disappear, leaving me and Kerrick alone.

I wiped the tears from my face and laid my head against his chest. He pulled me against him. It was a comforting gesture but felt somewhat stilted. Once again, he pushed me away and led me across the pasture to where the newly dug grave was located.

"Where did you sleep last night?" My voice quivered with emotion.

"The few hours I slept were in my cabin." He avoided looking at me. This was not Kerrick, my lover. This was the old Kerrick, the one who avoided emotion and attachment.

"Why did you leave me? I needed you, and you left me."

Pain shot across his face. "I failed you, Mickey. The first time you really needed me, and I was missing in action. It's the one thing I feared, and I can't live with that."

He couldn't live with that? I processed his words and then delivered my response. "You think you failed me because you couldn't save me from Morgan? No one could have saved me but me. It was the only way it could have played out. Don't you see that?" I stared at him in disbelief. "He would have waited for an opportunity to find me alone. What were you supposed to do? Quit your job and babysit me for the rest of your life?" Angry energy flowed though me, giving me the strength to continue. "You did fail me, but not because you weren't here. It happened because you were here and you pulled away. What happened to 'I'm not leaving?' You said you would never leave my bed or my side. You did both last night. You left me when I needed you the most."

His face fell as the truth of my words sank in. Did he not know how bad he would hurt me? I was assaulted, and my horse was murdered. All I wanted was to cling to something stable—to him. Could I be that bad of a judge of character? In all honesty, he'd warned me several times about his suitability for relationships. I should have listened.

"If you don't mind, I'd like some time alone. There's no risk of Morgan hurting me, so I no longer need you as a bodyguard."

"Mickey, I never meant to hurt you. I love you."

I sucked in a long, labored breath, and then exhaled. "I love you, too, Kerrick, but don't use me as an excuse for your inability to face your fears. You let me down, but I'm sure I could get over it if you were willing to work on it. What I can't get over is that you're failing yourself. This wasn't about your job. Your ex-wife gave you a prophecy, and your inability to see the truth of the situation has fulfilled it. I'm going to say it one more time, and then I'm moving on. I know Morgan better than anyone, and he would have figured out a way to get to me."

"Maybe, but—"

"No buts. I walked away from your brothers to visit my horse. If anyone was to blame, it was me. In Morgan's mind, I took something away from him, and he sought to do the same. Morgan won. He stole everything from me, including you. You're letting him win. Can't you see that?"

I turned away and walked up the hill without looking back. It was time to visit Mr. Darcy. With a handful of wildflowers I picked along the way, I placed them on the loose dirt covering the freshly dug grave. A rush of something fierce took over. I had spent too much time grieving. I'd grieved for the loss of my father, for the loss of my horses the first time, for the loss of my freedom, the cattle, the ranch, now Mr. Darcy *and* Kerrick. It would be difficult, but I'd overcome those losses. In the meantime, I'd move forward. I'd rather it be with Kerrick, but I'd do it without him if necessary.

Chapter 15

KERRICK

With my head hung low, I walked to my cabin to think. How did I mess this up so much? Things were going so well, and now... I wasn't trying to abandon her, I was giving her space. She lay rigid in my arms last night. It was like my touch bothered her. Given what happened to her, I feared she wouldn't want another man pawing at her.

I'd let my imagination get the best of me. I kept hearing my ex-wife's voice in my head, yelling things like, "You're never here when I need you." It was time to exorcise that woman from my head for good. The only woman I wanted screaming in my head was Mickey.

I went to my office Thursday but found that my heart wasn't in it. The job I'd loved so much seemed unimportant when compared to my love for Mickey. Back at the ranch, I created every situation I could think of to be near her.

For the next three days, I followed her around like a lovesick teen. I knew that I'd hurt her. She treated me with kindness and never once tossed a cross word in my direction. She was singularly focused on making the ranch work. She managed the property and my brothers with ease, and my respect for her grew.

It would have been easier if she had railed at me for something, at least then I'd know she cared enough to fight for me. The last few days, she'd been more reserved, less impulsive. Nothing had been decided on a whim. Everything had been thought out and considered. She adopted a pragmatic approach to everything she did. I missed the girl who flew by the seat of her pants.

"If you're going to mope, I don't want you in my barn." Keagan walked from behind a wall of hay bales.

"I'm not moping. I'm trying to figure things out." I combed my hand through my hair. "I gave her space, and now she doesn't trust me."

"I don't know what you did to her, but I want to kick your ass. She's the best thing that ever happened to you, to Killian, and me." My brother turned to me with a frown. "She's lost a lot in the last few years. Don't become another item on her list. I know you love her. I see it in everything you do." Keagan slapped me on the back and loaded hay on the trailer attached to the ATV.

"I do love her, and I want it to be good for us again, but I don't know what to do. I can't give her back what's been taken from her."

"No, you can give her something different. Give her something she's never experienced. Give her your unencumbered love, Kerrick."

"When did you get so smart?"

"I've been watching the Hallmark Channel. You can learn some good shit watching chick-flicks."

"You're watching Hallmark?"

His cheeks turned pink. "It's not my nightly ritual, but I like them. They're nice and leave you feeling good."

"Chocolate cake leaves me feeling good unless I eat too much of it. Then I get a bellyache."

"We aren't talking about chocolate cake. We're talking about Mickey, and she's worth the time it would take for you to get through one show."

"That's what you're using as dating advice? Hallmark?"

He chuckled. "You can tease me all you want, but one day some girl's going to cross my path, and I'll be prepared."

Set Free

"Some girl is going to cross your path, take one look at you, and cross the road to avoid you."

"Says the guy who had the perfect girl for a second."

Shaking my head, I headed to my cabin to plan. It was time I went after what I wanted.

Mickey was a small-town girl, but she wasn't Hallmark. She didn't need flowers and jewelry and poems. She needed someone who would be there. A man who would put her above all else. She needed him because he understood her. He sucked at communication, but he'd get better at that. Whatever Mickey needed was what he'd become. Because there was no way he'd spend the rest of his existence without her.

Chapter 16

MICKEY

It had been two days since I'd seen Kerrick. He took off in his truck and hadn't returned. The painful truth was, I might not be the woman to help him break free of his restricted outlook. Maybe it was too soon for him. Maybe it was the baggage I carried that kept him distant. The first few days after the incident, I thought he was going to approach me and ask me to talk. He didn't. He followed me around and stepped in to help with everything he could. He treated me like a fragile, wounded bird. Sure, wounded would be accurate, but never fragile. Something happened the minute I took Morgan down. It was as if the girl who cowered in fear had disappeared and a confident woman rose in her place.

Tired of watching everyone look at me with pity, I decided to set everything to rights over dinner. Whatever my issues were with Kerrick would in no way influence how I felt about the brothers. They were my new family, and I refused to give them up.

The men were scrubbing equipment when I entered the barn.

"Meeting in the main house, six o'clock. I'll make dinner." I turned around and marched home.

THE ENGINE of my truck roared to life. If I was feeding those two, I was going to need more food. The tires churned the dirt on the driveway. Dust billowed behind me.

Every time I entered the grocery store, I was filled with memories of Kerrick. I walked over to the peaches and bagged several before lifting one to my nose. The memory of him teasing me about tasting everything that smelled sweet was bittersweet.

The essentials to feed several ranch hands filled the cart: lots of meat, lots of starch and lots of beer. A couple pints of ice cream and a chocolate cake for later, and I was ready to check out. As luck would have it, I was in Lisa's line.

The cashier appeared wary of my presence. I could approach this situation in two ways: I could be nasty to the woman and punish her for her stupid choices, or I could embrace her, forgive her naiveté and empathize with her poor decisions.

"Hey, Lisa, how are you?" There was no use in holding grudges, life was too short. Hadn't I made the same mistake with Morgan?

Lisa appeared stunned at the friendly greeting. "I'm good, Mickey. It looks like you're having a cookout. What are you making? Brats?"

"Yep, I've got to feed the boys. They eat a lot." She rang up the groceries and bagged the food. It seemed like she wanted to say something. She started, then stopped, and started again.

"I...I...I gave Morgan the message. I'm sorry I didn't warn you. I was afraid." Her voice shrank with every word.

"Oh, listen, it's not your fault. I know what you were going through. I wish I could have warned you away from Morgan the first night I saw you. As it is, he's not going to be able to hurt either one of us ever again. I'm smarter because I lived through it. I hope you are as well. We've been given a second chance. I don't know about you, but I'm not wasting it."

"Thanks for being so understanding. I need to get smarter about the men I date. How's that hottie of yours?" That was the question of the moment. Not only how was he, but where was he?

"All the McKinley men are doing well." Not ready to discuss my personal life with Lisa, I moved the conversation forward. "What's my total?" Lisa sensed that our conversation had come to a close. She processed the payment and said goodbye.

At the ranch, I saw that Kerrick's truck had returned. My heart skipped a beat, knowing he was near. He always had that effect on me. However, with little time to spare, I fired up the grill for dinner.

The boys showed up at exactly six. I pulled the last brat off the grill and entered the house.

The two men sat silently at the table and waited.

"Eat. Don't let the brats get cold." I pushed a plate into each of their hands.

"Can I make a plate for Kerrick?" Killian asked. "He just got back."

I wondered where he'd been but didn't ask. "No, Kerrick is a big boy. If he wants to eat, he can come and get his own." It was about time he stopped hiding and showed up for his life again.

Keagan asked, "I'm not sure where he fits in here anymore, and I'm sure he's not sure either."

"Let's start this meeting now. First of all, so many things have happened in the last week. Losing my horse was devastating. Nothing is going to make that feel better. What's more, your brother walked away from me." I gave them both a *don't-interrupt-me* look when Keagan opened his mouth to speak. "I needed your brother after the event, and he bailed on me. I'd be willing to discuss it with him if he ever grew the balls to face me." Both men cringed at my attempt to emasculate Kerrick. Killian turned away, and Keagan tried to suppress his grin. How odd that he'd be laughing at a time like this.

"Mickey, he's suffering just like you are." Keagan wiped the smirk from his face. The earnest tone of his voice was touching. "You have to understand that his wife left him, because she said his job would get in the way of something important someday. Then you came along and worked your way into his heart. It was the first time he'd been happy in a long time. Then he went to work, and that bastard tried to kill you. He wasn't prepared for that." No one was prepared for Morgan. There was no way to prepare for him short of turning M and M Ranch into Fort Knox.

Set Free

"Neither was I, but I've let that asshole control my life for over three years, and he doesn't get another minute. He didn't almost kill me. He slapped me. He tripped me. He killed my horse. All of those things, I can and will recover from. I fought back, and thank God your brother put the shovel back where it belonged, because it saved me. So you see, he saved my life."

"Kerrick feels responsible." Keagan was sitting there, pressing for his brother, but where was his brother?

"I'm over it, and I want everyone else to get over it, too. I'm tired of living under a dark cloud. Either you get your happy faces back on, or find another place to live and work. I've become attached to both of you, so I hope you'll stay. Call your brother and tell him dinner is ready if he wants to eat."

Ten minutes later, there was a tentative knock on the door.

"Come in," I called out. "It's unlocked."

Kerrick walked in with a scowl on his face. He shut the door and turned the lock. "I'm not happy about that, Mickey." *Protective Kerrick was back.* Goosebumps rose on my arms. It was nice to see him again. No matter what happened, we had a connection, and until he went away, that connection was going to stay.

"Get over it, Kerrick. It's a ranch house. I like the door unlocked when I have several big, burly men hanging about. When I'm alone, I promise to be more careful, or maybe I'll get a boyfriend who wants to stick around and protect me." All eyes flashed to me. I knew my comment was snarky, but I felt compelled to say it. "Dinner is on the table. Help yourself."

Once everyone had their meal, I pulled out the ledgers and gave them an accounting of the financial health of the ranch. Everything was looking pretty good. We discussed next year's goals and decided to hire on at least one more person to help with the horses. Two more boarders had signed on, taking our paid numbers to lucky number thirteen. We also took in a stray today that was delivered while I was at the store. With thirteen paying clients, we could afford to take in a few homeless animals. Brody had one more breeding appointment, and the stallion would get to rest over the winter.

Kerrick sat at the table, listening to us and staring at the bowl of peaches in the center. I'd have given anything for his thoughts.

After cake and coffee were served, the younger McKinleys said thanks and headed home. Kerrick stayed behind on the premise of helping me clean up. He washed the dishes and wiped down the table.

"I've got laundry to do when you're finished with that," I teased. "You know, you don't have to clean my house to talk to me." This was a man I'd had an intimate relationship with, and he stood in my kitchen, acting like a teenage boy. He planted himself in front of me.

"I miss you. I'm sorry I wasn't there for you that night."

"Are we going to go over it again?" I sighed with exasperation. This conversation was exhausting.

"Stop. I'm talking about the night you thought I left you. I held you in my arms until three o'clock in the morning. I drowned in guilt that night. I went to my cabin as soon as I knew you were out for the night. The next morning, you were so mad. So hurt."

"My anger and hurt were caused by lots of things."

"I'm sorry. I don't want another minute to go by where we aren't together because of a misunderstanding. I realize I can't be your everything, but I can be your something."

"What do you want to be, Kerrick?" Tingles spread through my body. Was it possible that he'd finally come to his senses?

"I want to be yours. I want you to be mine." He leaned in, pushing me against the counter. With a gentle brush of his mouth, he touched my lips. He appeared to be testing the waters to see if it was a hospitable environment. *Could I do this again?* Could I take a chance on him? I thought I was done the first time he had walked away from me, but if I were being honest with myself, I'd never be done with him. He was like a virus that had invaded every one of my cells.

I turned my head to avoid his kiss, not to be mean, just to be clear.

"If you kiss me, it's a promise. When our lips touch, it's a pact that says I can depend on you, and you can count on me. It means when things get tough, and they will, neither of us will run. Your lips on mine is an oath, Kerrick, and if you can't commit to a relationship, then I don't want you to kiss me." He stood still, as if waiting for me to say more. Lucky for him, I had plenty to say. "I've spent my whole life around men who didn't value me—men, who disregarded my feelings. I'm not asking you to give up your job. I'm not asking you to be my savior. I'm asking you to be my partner. To walk with me, talk with me, hold my hand and listen. Give advice when it's warranted, stay quiet when it's wise. If you can't give me those things, then walk away."

His lips crushed into mine. My chest tightened with the knowledge that he was *all in* this time. The loneliness of the last two weeks was replaced with hope for the future.

We stumbled to the bedroom, shedding clothes as we went. Desperation to connect with one another overshadowed any sexual finesse we may have possessed. We fell into bed, a jumble of naked limbs. When the head of his hardness slipped inside me, I moaned with satisfaction, remembering how good it felt to have him become one with me. Making love had never been so gratifying.

We lay sated and sweaty in each other's arms. It was where I wanted to be. It was where I should have been all along. It was where I planned to be in the future.

"I'm going to need your cabin," I said as I snuggled into his side.

"Are you evicting me?" He turned toward me so we were face to face. Our legs naturally intertwined with each other.

"Yes, Holly is coming soon, then I hope Megan, Natalie, and Robyn will follow. I need to hire one, maybe two more hands. Add your brothers to the mix, and the cabins are full. There's no room for you. Besides, I want you here, next to me. You belong with me."

"I do, and I promise I'll never leave your side again."

Flowery words camouflaged intention. "I don't want your promise. Promise is just a word. It holds no meaning. I'd rather be convinced by your actions, than disappointed by your words. Convince me, Kerrick."

He leaned forward and kissed me, his soft lips warm against mine. The kiss was both tender and firm. I wanted for him to take me again, to claim me.

"Mine. You're mine," he growled. Those words, although only words, took my breath away. Maybe there was power in words, but it was his actions that truly twisted my heart. I wrapped my arms around him. Would I ever get enough of him? I longed for this moment. Every part of me came alive at his touch. I tried to crawl into his body. I needed him to be as close to me as possible. We connected in the most intimate way possible. Buried inside me, he made love to me with passion. Every stroke, every kiss was a soothing balm to heal my wounded heart.

I woke the next morning with his arm wrapped around my waist.

"Good morning, Sugar."

I scooted as close as I could to him. My muscles were sore, my mind and body content. "Hmmm," I purred. "What time is it?"

"It's after eight." He held me tight, holding me down so I couldn't bolt from the bed. "The horses have been taken care of this morning. Your only job is to lay here and let me hold you."

"Hmmm, I think I can do that." And I did. I lay in his arms the entire day and night. The only time we left each other was to bathe and eat. Right before I dozed, I thought, *Perfect moments sometimes come from imperfection.*

A domino effect had ruled my life for the last three years. Who would have thought that a parent's death could lead to a bad relationship, a stint in prison, a kind gesture from a stranger, a new purpose, and a grand love? I realized I was offered an encore performance in my life, and I intended to earn a standing ovation for my future efforts.

The next day, Kerrick got me up bright and early. I asked if his brothers could deal with the horses, but he said no. He informed me that Keagan sent a text requesting my presence in the stables right away.

Filled with panic, I hopped out of bed, visited the bathroom, threw on clothes, and dashed out the door. My first thoughts were that maybe we didn't locate the remaining oleander and another horse was sick.

"Hold up, Sugar. He didn't say it was an emergency." His even tone calmed me. If there were a problem, they would have called me directly. Feeling better, I wrapped my hand in Kerrick's, and we strolled to the stables.

He dropped my hand and walked ahead of me. All three McKinleys stood next to Mr. Darcy's stall. I didn't know what they were up to, but it couldn't be good. If it took three of them, then it was a big deal. I rounded the corner and came face to face with what could have been a clone of Mr. Darcy, only this horse was female.

Tears sprang to my eyes, and all three men panicked. "I'm not sad." I wiped the tears and walked toward the mare. "What's her name?"

Kerrick stepped forward. "We registered her under the name Darcy's Pride, but you can call her whatever you want."

My heart filled with joy. "Darcy's Pride is perfect. Where did you get her?"

"Dr. Mallory located the ranch where Mr. Darcy came from. She's bred from the same set of parents. She's five years old. We hope you like her." The three men stared at me.

"I think I'm going to love her. I can't believe you all conspired together to hoodwink me. Shame on you, but I love you all the more for doing it. How did you sneak her in? I had no idea."

Kerrick pulled me into his arms. I barely noticed that his brothers had left us alone.

"I drove to Idaho to pick her up, but I'd have traveled anywhere to get her for you. We waited for you to leave long enough to sneak her into the stables. Thank goodness you decided to grocery shop. Our last ditch plan was to walk her onto the property in the dead of the night."

Never had I expected to be loved and cherished like that in my life. I felt complete. Content. Amazed.

"You did all this for me? What did I do to deserve this?"

"You loved me, Mickey."

Chapter 17

KEAGAN

The horn continued to blow from the approaching truck. Killian and I filed out of our cabins to see what all the fuss was about. Mickey pulled her truck in front of cabin six.

"What the hell is going on?" Killian asked.

"It's Mickey and her ex-convict friend. I love Mickey, but I'm not sure I want to raise horses next to criminals." I wasn't convinced that a ranch full of criminals would be good for any of us.

"Mickey came from the jail." Killian's statement was short, but it was Killian's style—short on words, powerful delivery. He was right, Mickey did come from prison, but she was not the villain I'd have imagined an ex-convict to be.

Killian was deeply loyal to our boss. It was a good thing Kerrick had staked his claim on Mickey; otherwise, Killian might have fallen head over heels for her. Why did men lose their heads over women? I'd never let a woman come between my horses and me. Love was fine for others, but I didn't have time for it.

Mickey jumped from the truck, looking radiant and happy. She ran to the side and called for our help.

"Looks like Holly is going to need a place to live after all. Can you help carry her things into the cabin? It took us all morning to

Set Free

get them from her old place. We're exhausted." She gave us a *move-your-ass* look, and we both stepped to it.

I took a basket of clothes and walked toward the door just as the passenger side swung open. One shapely leg followed the other while she slid from the seat. My eyes traveled up the long, smooth limbs to a pair of cut-off shorts, a set of luscious round breasts, and the most beautiful woman with a halo of blonde hair. I dropped the basket. "I'm so screwed."

NEXT up is *Set Aside*

A Sneak Peek at Set Aside

Outside the prison, I sat and waited. Liberation felt overwhelmingly lonely. For the first time in decades, I'd face the world alone, and that frightened the hell out of me.

Thankfully, the universe was finally showing me a hint of a smile, and my heart thawed in the uncharacteristically warm October air. The sun was out, and the birds were singing, whistling freedom's ballad. It was funny how the birds sang outside the prison, but I'd never heard them on the other side of the fence.

Everything appeared softer, more inviting on this side of the yard. From where I sat, even the chain-link didn't seem as tall or foreboding. With my arms wrapped around my shins, and my chin on my knees, I watched the empty road ahead. Mickey was expected at eleven. I waited, inhaling the scent of car exhaust and grass clippings, the sweet scent of liberty. They were a welcome respite from the stale prison enclosure.

Around and around, I rolled my shoulders. A restless night in my bunk had left me with a stiff neck. My last night in prison, and it covered the spectrum of best and worst nights of my existence. Best because it was my last night, worst because I couldn't lie in my bunk anymore and dream about my future. I had to create one, and I had no idea where to begin. All I knew was, I must begin.

In the distance, a dust cloud rolled up the road. A hint of blue peeked through the nebulous dirt ball, a horn blared, and the smile I'd been missing since she was released from Cell Block C was there. With the finesse of a race car driver, the truck did a perfect donut and came to a stop in front of me.

"Hey, do you need a ride?"

"Let me think." I hopped from the cement steps, ready to go. "I could enjoy a lunch of mystery meat on hard bread, or I could have you take me for a burger." I gave her a *what-do-you-think?* look. "Gosh, Mickey, that is such a tough decision." I raced away from the prison toward the truck, toward the only friend I had outside the fence. "You were supposed to be here fifteen minutes ago." I teased, knowing full well she was early.

"You are so full of shit." She gave me a *get your ass in the truck* smirk while she eyed the small purse in my hand. "Do you need help with your luggage?"

I tossed the leather pouch at her head.

She ducked.

"Good dodge. I wouldn't want you to get a concussion from the sheer size and weight of my bag."

"Get in the truck, Holly; we've got shit to do."

It took about six seconds for Mickey to yank her buckle free and throw her arms around me once I entered the truck.

"Holy shit...are you really here?"

For the first time in months, I breathed freely. "Yep, I made it. Now comes the hard stuff." I held on to Mickey for way too long, but I felt if I let her go, she might disappear. I had missed her more than I thought possible.

Mickey pulled away and wiped at the tears pouring down her face.

"I'm so glad you're here. I have your cabin ready. Your letter said you weren't moving in with Matt. Tell me what happened. I wanted you to have your happily ever after. Lord knows we spent enough time in the bunks planning your life. We plotted it out so perfectly. You would live in your high rise apartment with your 2.5 children and ugly nanny. Holly, what happened?" Mickey's soft demeanor would change the minute I told her the truth about Matt. Mickey was a fierce and loyal friend.

"I'm not quite sure, but I have some suspicions, and I need to confirm them. Are you willing to help me catch the asshole red-handed?"

"I'm down for whatever you need. What are we up against?"

"I'm just looking for a few truths. Stuff doesn't make sense, and yet...it does. I'll know when I get there."

"I'm game. It's hard to believe you're the same girl they said wouldn't utter a profanity when she entered the system." Mickey snapped her buckle in place and grabbed the steering wheel. "Let's blow this hellhole."

I leaned over and turned the volume of the radio up, effectively ending our conversation about Matt. "I love this song." I swayed to the beat of the music.

"How is it you know modern music? I finished my sentence, which was half of yours, and I didn't know a damn thing playing on the radio." She grumbled something about music and fairness.

"It was a perk of working in the kitchen. We had a radio. Roz was partial to the oldies, but every Friday she played the top forty station as a reward for our hard work. It was our consolation prize for having to serve fish sticks."

She put the car into gear and eased down the road. "Where to, doll? I'm at your service." I turned around and watched my past fade from view.

"Take the freeway to Broadway, and then take exit 207A. The address is 2715 Broadway, Apt 2B."

"I could have called him to tell him we were coming. He could have had your stuff ready."

Duh. "If you're trying to catch a thief, you don't tell them you're coming. Same with a cheating, lying bastard."

"Oh my God, the asshole's been cheating on you? He doesn't know you're coming? Holy shit." Slack-jawed, she continued to drive. Her hands gripped the steering wheel, and her knuckles turned white.

"I didn't think he could keep it in his pants. I told him to break it off with me, but he said he would wait. Hell, I was so naive when I entered prison. I actually let him convince me." A laugh escaped, and I wondered if I'd lost my mind.

"Asshole." Mickey laid her hand on the horn and released a ribbon of colorful words at the driver who had cut her off. "Let me tell you, Holly, drivers haven't gotten better while you were in prison. I think the government released something in the air that sucked out people's brains."

Her mention of the brain had me thinking about the loss of my RN license. I reminded myself to grab my NCLEX study guide from the bookshelf when we got to Matt's.

"Lots of areas of the brain are engaged when driving, Mickey. The parietal lobe deals with spatial relations while the occipital and temporal lobes deal with both visual and auditory. Then there's the cerebellum . . ."

"You are way too fucking smart for your own fucking good." Mickey reached over and slapped at my arm.

"You're smart, too. You would sound smarter if every other word wasn't an expletive. What the heck, Mick? You're worse now than you were in prison. One thing I learned while there was that a carefully placed *fuck you* had a lot more power than a string of profanities." I shifted my head slowly back and forth. She really needed to clean up her act.

"Don't give me shit. I work with men on a ranch, and Kerrick likes my dirty mouth," her wet tongue slid out to ring her lips, "especially when it's wrapped around his—."

I slapped my hands over my ears and yelled, "Stop. I don't want to hear about Kerrick's penis."

"Oh, please, like I'd use that word. I was going to say co—"

"Christ. Cut me some slack. It's not like I've had the pleasure in two years."

"I'm sure you heard about lots of cocks in prison. I think Roz served it on Fridays, only she breaded them and passed them off as

A Sneak Peek at Set Aside

fish sticks. Right before I left, Officer Brady walked in the kitchen like the big dick he was and ran out like a pussy. What happened that day?"

I laughed at the memory.

"Officer Brady was tired of fish sticks. He came into the kitchen and told Roz to serve another meat. She told him that she had no other options. He grabbed his crotch and tugged, telling her he had some meat for her. She went for her cleaver, and he went for the door. Brady never came around the kitchen again."

"I wondered what went down that day. He always made an effort to steer clear of Roz. For an old buzzard, she managed to scare the hell out of the toughest guards. They gave her a wide berth."

Thoughts of Roz made me smile. "Did you know she was a prisoner for five years? When she finished her sentence, she applied for the kitchen manager's position. She's been there ever since—like twenty years. I couldn't imagine working there once I was released, but it showed me there was a future beyond the walls. She gave me hope."

Through the windshield, my old apartment building came into view. My heart pounded in my chest. Blood boomed like thunder in my ears. I wasn't sure I was ready for the confrontation, and yet it had to be done.

"Are you ready to do this thing?" Mickey threw the truck in park and stepped out. She'd never been this confident in jail. Freedom had done her good. Kerrick had done her good. I would never have pegged her as someone who would have hooked up with a cop. Life was exactly like fiction, strange.

Still used to being told when to walk, where to walk, hell, even how to walk, I moved slower. "It's now or never." Matt would sure be surprised that I showed up at our door a week earlier than expected.

When I met her out in front of the steps, Mickey cracked her knuckles like she was my strong-arm. "What do you think we're going to find?"

"If his schedule is the same, he'll be home. What I expect to find is someone else besides him." I pressed the button for 2B, took my keys out of my bag and snapped opened the lobby door. "Whatever slut he's been hooking up with." As the door closed, Matt's voice sounded over the intercom.

"Hello...hello...is anyone—"

The door clicked closed and silenced his voice.

Walking toward my former home, it felt as if the last two years had never happened. Same cracked floor tiles and broken mailboxes. Same slow ride up to the second floor. Same faded brown door that used to welcome me home. I closed my eyes. But two years had happened. Everything was different. I was different. I rapped on the door.

His footsteps thundered across the wooden floor. The door handle shook. A shadow crossed the peephole.

Nothing. Absolute silence.

I rapped again, only this time with more force. The deadbolt shifted. The door opened.

The color rushed from his face. "Holly." He stumbled back a step as if I were there to do him bodily harm, which wouldn't be out of bounds if busting his nose wouldn't send me back to prison. "Why didn't you tell me you were getting out early?" His gaze scanned the room like a guard looking for contraband.

"I wanted it to be a surprise." I skimmed my hand down his face as I walked past him and into my old home. It could be so easy to go back to status quo, but that was no longer an option. I wanted more from my life.

"It's definitely a surprise. A great surprise." He looked around the room and zoned in on Mickey.

"Matt, this is Mickey. She's one of my best friends from prison."

Mickey nodded and leaned against the wall. She didn't say a word. Her contribution to keeping him off kilter.

"Hi, Mickey." His greeting had the emotional equivalent of a piece of wood—hard and splintered. "Great to meet you." He wrapped his arms around my waist and put his sweet on. "Always loved these shorts. They're a cross between Daisy Dukes and cargo pants. My kind of perfect woman."

Before prison, his breath grazing my neck would have sent chills all the way down to my curlies, but now my butt clenched. With a clean twist, I outmaneuvered him and headed for the living room. The apartment was the same and not...it smelled different than the gardenia candles I'd burned. Now hairspray, lemon cleaner, and a cloyingly sweet perfume stank the room. I walked around, touching the things we used to share. Bookshelves full of medical journals filled one wall, but things were missing, too. Picture frames that used to hold our photos had disappeared. I thought I would feel sad walking into my *what could have been* life. I expected it to feel like a punch to the gut. All I felt was empty.

On the bottom shelf, my favorite nursing book was gone. Like I was never a part of this existence. Over the last two years, I'd been erased and replaced. Set aside.

"Where's my book?" My tone was direct and to the point. I was here for two things. The first was to get what belonged to me, and the second was to set free what was no longer mine.

"I put them away." He rocked on his feet. "I'll get them for you later." He paced the room. "How does it feel to be home?" His voice broke like a teenage boy.

This...home? I shook my head. Home was where the people who love you lived. Where you didn't have to be anyone but yourself. A place where you had value. How sad I had to be reminded of that in prison.

"It will feel better when I get these clothes off. Come on, Mickey, help me find something nice to wear."

Matt's face tumbled at the mention of clothes. I dragged Mickey down the hall to the bedroom that once had been Matt's and mine. Matt nipped at our heels. I knew my books weren't the only things that had been packed away, but watching Matt sweat gave me joy.

The lime green and orange pillows on the bed screamed shitty taste. Shitty taste wasn't Matt. He might be a selfish bastard, but good taste was something he always had.

"Holly, please..." He pushed himself in front of us, blocking the closet door.

"Save it, Matt. I know. I just needed confirmation."

His mouth dropped open, and I wondered if his reaction was because I knew, or because I hadn't killed him yet?

"It wasn't supposed to happen like this. Everything would have been back to normal by next week. It wasn't my intention to hurt you, to make you feel bad." His excuse was like Kool-Aid poured into a wine bottle. The color was pleasing, but the taste failed.

Mickey shoved him aside and yanked open the closet. "She doesn't feel bad; she feels free."

Matt gaped. "You gotta understand." His voice was whiney. "Everything would have been fine if you had stuck to the schedule." He deflated the minute Mickey stepped inside the closet.

Mickey rummaged through the hoochie mama dresses she would know weren't mine. She pulled a pair of jeans from the hanger and pressed them to my waist. Six inches too short. She spun on him. "Dr. Becker is it? I suggest you direct us toward her belongings. I spent a year in prison and almost killed my ex when I got out. I can't imagine what two years does to a girl."

"Right." He jumped like Mickey had lit his ass on fire. "I have your boxes down in the storage locker. Unfortunately, your Jeep isn't here. I can have it by tonight, if that's okay."

"You let someone borrow my Jeep? What the hell is wrong with you?" I could overlook someone in my bed. Letting someone borrow my car was another matter. "I want my Jeep back today, Matt. I also want my book. Who the hell needed my nursing book?" As soon as the words were out of my mouth, I knew who. Maybe not the exact person, but she'd be a nurse, and she'd be using my books and my Jeep, and that thought pissed me off.

"Holly, I'm sorry." His was a feeble apology. There was no muscle behind it; just the weak words of a liar.

"Mickey can tell you where I live. I haven't been there yet."

"We won't be home tonight," she damn near snarled. "We're celebrating, Rick's Roost for dinner and tequila shots. You'll have to make other arrangements." Her demeanor was sharp enough to cut paper.

"I know where Rick's Roost is; I'll meet you there, and we can all celebrate. The more, the merrier, right? Have you called any of your friends from the hospital? Carla is dying to see you."

"I just want my Jeep. As for Carla, I'll call her. Is she still in the same job—my job?"

His eyes looked around the room.

I glanced around, trying to see what he did. There was a romance novel on the nightstand, a bottle of perfume on the dresser, and a thong hanging from the drawer.

"Yes, she's the shift supervisor in the ER. She was next in line, and when you left, she was placed in the position right away." His face looked constipated, like he wanted to push out something too painful to pass. "How did you know?"

I walked over to the dresser and picked up the bottle of perfume. I spritzed a bit into the air and turned to walk away. "I smelled another woman's scent on you."

He ushered us out the door and into the elevator. "I got caught over a twenty dollar bottle of perfume." His shoulders shook as he laughed. Glad he could find humor in such a shitty situation.

"Bring my Jeep and my book to Rick's Roost tonight. Bring your girlfriend, I'd love to meet her. You can buy a round for everyone. We'll toast to new beginnings."

Mickey gave me a *you have to be kidding* look.

Matt had the smile of a kid who just got his way. I've always had a soft spot for his smile, and today was no different. He was a jerk, but he was a jerk with nice teeth.

Mickey shrugged her shoulders. "Why not? The bar is full of assholes. The more the merrier."

Matt helped us load several boxes into the bed of the truck. He pulled me into his arms and held me a little too long. I pushed away and hightailed it to my side of the truck. He followed.

"How do you want to split our stuff? I had an appraiser come in and give me an estimate when I updated the insurance. I'm happy to pay you for half. It would make my life so much easier. I'll even add an extra ten percent for the time it took you to pick out the stuff." He pleaded with me to say yes.

"That's fine Matt, whatever you think is fair." That response was an echo of the old Holly, the one who went with the flow and didn't ruffle feathers, but a clean break would be good, and I could use the money.

Mickey grumbled something like *Let's go* before she hopped in the truck and revved the engine.

"Ms. Impatient is ready. It's good to see you, Matt. I hope you're happy."

"Holly, you've changed. And those changes are attractive. Maybe we could revisit the thing we had. There is something incredibly sexy about your newfound confidence. You know, I think I could be happier." He moved in to kiss me, but I placed my hand on his chest, halting his progress.

"You're the past, and there's nowhere for you in my future."

Get a free book.

Go to www.authorkellycollins.com

Other Books by Kelly Collins

The Second Chance Series
Set Free

Set Aside

Set in Stone

Set Up

Set on You

The Second Chance Series Box Set

The Boys of Fury Series
Redeeming Ryker

Saving Silas

Delivering Decker

The Boys of Fury Boxset

About the Author

International bestselling author of more than thirty novels, Kelly Collins writes with the intention of keeping love alive. Always a romantic, she blends real-life events with her vivid imagination to create characters and stories that lovers of contemporary romance, new adult, and romantic suspense will return to again and again.

For More Information
www.authorkellycollins.com
kelly@authorkellycollins.com

Acknowledgments

I want to thank my street team for all the help they offer.

For all the cowboys I've stopped and probed for answers, you are amazing. For the cowgirl I met at the nail salon, thanks for being so generous with your time.

Mostly, thanks to all the fans that buy my books and pass the word, without you…there's no reason to write.

Printed in Great Britain
by Amazon